CU00933267

All rights reserved.

No part of this publication may be sold, copied, distributed, reproduced or transmitted in any form or by any means, mechanical or digital, including photocopying and recording or by any information storage and retrieval system without the prior written permission of both the publisher, Oliver Heber Books and the author, Carla Simpson, except in the case of brief quotations embodied in critical articles and reviews.

PUBLISHER'S NOTE: This is a work of fiction. Names, characters, places, and incidents either are the product of the author's imagination or are used fictitiously. Any resemblance to actual persons, living or dead, business establishments, events, or locales is entirely coincidental.

A Deadly Scandal Copyright © 2024 Carla Simpson

Cover art by Dar Albert at Wicked Smart Designs

Published by Oliver-Heber Books

0 9 8 7 6 5 4 3 2 1

Prologue

THE LARGE HOUSE with wings that spread across the grounds like those of a large bird was mostly silent now, except for the occasional glow of an electric light as a servant went about the last of his duties for the night.

There had been cloud cover earlier, but wind had picked up, and now the moon slipped out from behind a cloud and lit the vast gardens at Sandringham in gray hues that spread to the forest beyond.

The pathway disappeared as he made his way to the tree line as he had before, to that arranged meeting place.

A glance back over his shoulder and he slipped into the dense tree cover, the piney scent surrounding him as moonlight disappeared with dense foliage, then reappeared in slivers of light that spilled onto the forest floor, guiding his footsteps.

This was the end of it. Afterward, he thought, he would return to London with the others after the long weekend of gaming and hunting, and none would be the wiser for this final journey into the forest and what he had decided must be done.

It had nothing to do with the money—he had enough to live very comfortably wherever he chose, from a family inheritance. It had everything to do with the person waiting for him when it was finally done. A daring and dangerous plan that had been set in motion the previous year and now quickened his footsteps.

Was he prepared for the inevitable calamity it would cause after a brilliant military career that brought a wall full of meaningless medals? After orders that had ended in the deaths of countless good men? And the return to a life that had become empty and meaningless?

The weekend in Sandringham House with his Royal Highness and his circle of friends was part of it, the final step that would buy him time. No one would suspect anything until long after it was done, and by then he would be gone.

There were words that would describe the choice he made and what he had done, but that would all be left behind when he disappeared and became someone else.

It had already been arranged months earlier and now there was just this final step to be taken.

He reached the clearing that he had discovered on that previous weekend excursion of hunting and gaming.

With the village of Sandringham very near the Norfolk coast, it was the perfect location and the last piece that had fallen into place, waiting only to be set in motion.

He frowned as he entered the clearing and that other figure stepped from the shadows. There was a smile, so very sweet.

"It is late. I was afraid you might have been discovered."

"I had to wait until the others had retired for the night."

"Do you have it?"

"Of course...!" he replied, then hesitated. "I thought that he would be here. Has there been a change of plans?"

A shake of the head and the hood of the mantle slipped to his companion's shoulders, revealing silvery-gold hair.

"*Non,*" came the accented response. "Our friend is too well known and it was decided that no one would suspect a woman."

He understood, although he didn't care for the change in the plans. No word had been sent.

"Very well," he replied. The only thing left was to give the woman the package he had brought with him. He handed it to her.

She immediately opened the thick envelope and inspected the contents.

"It is all there," he told her with irritation along with a growing uneasiness.

Organization and precision were long-established habits acquired in his former career and often meant the difference between life and death on the field of battle. Last-minute changes could be reckless and dangerous.

"What of the rest of it?" He didn't bother to disguise his displeasure.

She tucked that thick envelope into the folds of the long cloak she wore, then looked up and replied in that same accent.

"Nothing else has changed."

It might have been that smile that slowly faded, the expression that narrowed in her eyes. Or it might have been that sudden stirring in the branches of the tree behind him after the wind had died down—a warning that slipped through the shadows.

"Do it!" she ordered.

He gasped, thrust his arms out as reality set in, then gasped again. In a matter of seconds, it was over.

He was slowly lowered to the ground, mouth gaping open

in stunned surprise. But there were no words, only that last gasping sound as blood seeped out onto the floor of the forest...

One

OLD LODGE, SCOTLAND

THE CONTRAST of Scotland to the Sahara was startling, with its jagged slate peaks, the marshy bogs, double rainbows on late misty mornings, and the thick pine forest.

It could also be wild, forbidding, just as primitive in its own way, yet it was a refuge of sorts, a place where I had been raised as a child, along with the more cultured environs of London and other far places that I had traveled.

But it was here where I could pull on trousers and tall boots and lose myself to the calming silence amidst the rolling hills that lay beneath those jagged peaks.

Usually.

"Look what I found!"

My companion for my morning hike through the forest came running quite excited along the path we followed. Old Lodge, that formidable old hunting lodge, was tucked into the base of one of those peaks. With its legends and stories of smugglers, highwaymen, and that spectacular whisky distillery my great-aunt's father had established some years before.

It was also a place of hasty decisions. My own, that is, in

what appears to have possibly been a rash moment, and I am not usually given to rash moments.

The north of Scotland could be unpredictable due to the changing season, and the roads which were almost non-existent when rain set in for days at a time.

It had been overcast most of the morning, the clouds pulling back at midday, then returning by late afternoon with that misty rain that was referred to as a fine soft rain.

That *fine soft rain* had soaked us both.

"What have you there?" I asked Lily, my ward, who had traveled to the Sahara these months past with my great-aunt and me.

She had been born in Scotland, although the year and her true family were mostly unknown. We had met during a previous inquiry case when she had worked as a lady's maid in an Edinburgh brothel known as the Church, and had surprisingly provided assistance. Not to mention that she had undoubtedly saved my life, or in the very least assisted Brodie in the matter that led to the solving of the case.

Afterward, I refused to simply leave her to the one prospect for her future in a brothel, and offered to bring her to London, provide an education, and hopefully a future far different from the one in the Church. She had eventually accepted my offer.

So here we were, trudging along the footpath together back to Old Lodge. I had taken her to all my old favorite places to explore in the woods. It did appear that she had retrieved something from the gap in the base of the juniper tree where I had gone exploring at very much her age. Although sadly, she had no way of knowing what her true age was.

"*It was what mistress at the Church told me when I first went to live there,*" she had said with a shrug at the time.

It was as close to being a mother as I would ever get, after being told I could never bear children after a particularly nasty illness as a child. And I was quite agreeable with that, as I had never been fond of infants no matter whom they belonged to.

A shortcoming, for certain, for most women. However, the truth was that I enjoyed having Lily as part of our somewhat unconventional family that consisted of my sister, the two of us orphaned quite young, then raised by our great-aunt who had never wed or had other family.

Although not for lack of prospects, as they say. She explained that she had simply never found a man worth attaching herself to, as she put it. I was not certain of that, and suspected that there may have been one particular man along the way. However, it seemed that nothing had come of it.

And to be honest my great-aunt was quite...unique. At eighty-six years of age, she had traveled extensively, lived quite well. She was rumored to be wealthier than the Queen, and didn't give a fig what anyone said or thought about the more colorful aspects of her life.

I adored her, and it had been said on more than one occasion that we had a great deal in common.

She had lived long enough to experience a great many things, had acquired a considerable amount of wisdom along the way, was unusually curious, and could be fearless when adventuring or learning about new things.

Except for the 'damned telephone,' as she referred to it—noisy, bothersome, and people wanted to talk on it all day long. Didn't they have anything else to do?

Such as building a jungle in her solar, complete with a monkey, so that she could prepare for our safari. Or having a replica of the River Nile in Egypt built in the grand hall at her home at Sussex Square for a celebration.

All these months later, the boat was still there.

"Quite unique and exciting, don't you think?" she had replied when asked if she intended to have it removed.

After all, who else had a full-size Egyptian sailboat found on the Nile in the middle of their great hall? And on more than one occasion she could be found taking afternoon *'tea,'* which in truth was some of the whisky distilled at Old Lodge.

I often joined her there, particularly after returning from Egypt and the Sahara on our recent safari.

"And how is Mr. Brodie?"

My answers had been quite inventive and invariably the same:

He was undoubtedly quite busy with an inquiry case.

He had taken on some additional responsibilities with Rory, a young boy orphaned in our previous inquiry.

Or, the counterfeit case we had both worked on had taken a great deal of his time.

And then, it seemed that he was in the midst of trying to find another location for the office, since the building on the Strand had apparently been sold. I had learned this from Munro, his long-time friend who was my aunt's estate manager.

When I ran out of excuses, I started over again. Not that it fooled my great-aunt.

The truth was that I had no idea how he was, other than the few very brief comments from Munro that I had been able to pry out of him. He was, after all, a Scot—they could be most reserved and reticent, as I knew only too well.

"I have not seen him in some days," became a frequent response from Munro to my carefully worded comments about this or that in an attempt to learn more about what Brodie was up to.

The truth was there had been a serious falling-out between us during our last inquiry case. It was afterward that I had joined my great-aunt and Lily on their travels. I decided there was a need for some distance between Brodie and me in order to figure out some things—most particularly, our relationship.

When we returned, over a month earlier, there had been no contact from him, no inquiry regarding our adventure in the Sahara, no note to acknowledge that we had even returned...nothing.

It did seem that the anger and harsh words of that last disagreement had turned to indifference.

Lily was breathless as she caught up with me.

"Maybe there's word from Mr. Brodie today."

Having never known her father or any other family, she had grown quite fond of him during our 'arrangement,' that now seemed as if it might be in jeopardy.

"I'll show him what I found," she added with a sideways glance.

The girl was far too observant and clever.

She now opened her hand to show me the 'treasure' she had found rummaging around among the trees, rocks and hidden places, as we trudged back toward the lodge where I hoped a warm fire and a dram of whisky was waiting.

We stopped as we reached the gate the led up the flagstone walk to the Lodge. Her *treasure* was a medallion in the shape of a heart, but badly tarnished. It appeared to be of silver with the design of a thistle and a stag's head.

"Do ye think it was lost by a smuggler?" she asked excitedly. Smugglers and highwaymen were a favorite topic.

Anything was possible since the Lodge had been standing for more than three hundred years, certainly long enough for a smuggler to have traveled through. And there were all those old stories that my great-aunt had told my sister and me when we were children.

"Oh, my," my great-aunt said as Lily told her of her discovery and handed her the medallion.

My great-aunt softly smiled then stroked the medallion with her fingers. "It's called a '*Luckenbooth*,'" she told Lily.

She turned it over in her fingers. "It was given as a token between two lovers upon their betrothal."

"It will be quite lovely when it's polished," she continued, and I could have sworn there was a soft catch in her voice.

She handed it back to Lily. "You have made a marvelous discovery, my dear."

"Ye might give it to Mr. Brodie, when ye see him," Lily suggested to me.

That seemed unlikely, considering our last parting.

"There is mail on the side table," my great-aunt then mentioned, changing the subject quite handily as she continued.

"I opened a letter from your sister. It was over two weeks old. It seems that Mr. Warren has proposed. Lenore has thoughts about a springtime wedding; however, Mr. Warren has suggested Christmas," she continued. "He does seem quite eager."

James Warren was the publisher of my novels. He had been most excited about taking on my author career after I had encountered some...shall we call it opposition, even condescending attitudes from other publishers who, I had always suspected, took meetings with me in deference to my great-aunt's standing.

Mr. Warren had been enthusiastic and most eager for additional books, and I liked him very much. I had 'arranged' for him and my sister to meet. They did seem perfect for one another.

"The time is quite short," my aunt continued. "It would

require some rather quick planning. However, it will make the Holidays most exciting."

I smiled to myself. I did wonder if that might include a sail down the River Nile at Sussex Square. I had poured myself a dram of my great-aunt's whisky, and the feeling had finally returned to my toes.

The planning of a wedding most certainly would give her something to do after the excitement of our recent travels.

"Oh, and there is a telegram that the boy from the village delivered along with the mail," she added. "It's there on top of the letters."

A telegram? Was it possible that it was from Brodie?

I downed the rest of the whisky and casually approached the table. When what I wanted to do was snatch it up, take it to my room, and tear it open.

It was addressed quite formally, and I felt a sudden disquiet. It was the sort of missive that might be sent from an administrator or possibly...an attorney. It was addressed: *Lady Mikaela Forsythe, Old Lodge, Inveresk, Scotland.*

Brodie had been so very angry when we had argued. Was it possible that he had decided to end our marriage.

My hands shook...

Two

"*ARE you going to open it, or merely stare at it?*" my aunt asked in her very direct way.

Also, in her very direct way, she had left no doubt as to her opinion regarding my decision to accompany her on safari.

"*Out of concern for my well-being, my foot!*" she told me at the time, when I had announced my intention to accompany her.

"*And what of Mr. Brodie?*"

I had explained, somewhat vaguely, that he needed some time to recover from that recent inquiry case and his injuries, and left it at that. However, not one to be subtle or to let the matter lie...she had made a more recent comment regarding my residence at Mayfair and his very obvious absence from an occasional visit to Sussex Square.

"*I would imagine that Mr. Brodie should have sufficiently recovered by now. If not, he may have succumbed. However, I have not read of it in the death notices. Hmmm?*"

I had replied that I was certain he had recovered, although my source for that was Munro.

And then there were her musings on the nature of men in general, from her vast experience.

"*Men can be somewhat difficult at times even to the point of stubbornness. I do believe there must be something in the blood that makes them so, Scots particularly,*" she had added pointedly.

I continued to stare at the envelope. The flap had been sealed by the telegraph operator. I quickly opened it and pulled out the telegram. Best to get this over with, I thought.

However, in my wildest musings, I was not at all prepared for what it contained.

Lady Forsythe.

Urgent that you return at once to London without delay. Your assistance is required. Contact me immediately upon your arrival.

Sir Avery Stanton, Special Services Agency, London

"Bloody hell."

"Is there something wrong, dear?" my great-aunt asked.

My assistance was required?

It did seem that Brodie was apparently well and alive—it certainly wasn't notification of any catastrophe in that regard.

Therefore, there was only one reason Sir Avery had sent that telegram.

I had, after all, made that agreement months earlier...an agreement that had driven the wedge even further between Brodie and me.

It did seem that *wedge* was an understatement. His reaction had been explosive and seemingly quite final.

I suppose there was no choice in the matter. I might refuse, but I had visions of Sir Avery sending some of his 'people' to retrieve me if I didn't make a timely appearance.

"It seems that I must return to London," I finally replied, not at all pleased about it. I could only imagine what it was that *required* my assistance.

I insisted that Lily remain at Old Lodge with my great-aunt. No sense in shortening their stay on my account,

"Sir Avery Stanton?" my aunt had inquired of the telegram. She had remarkable eyesight for someone her age, given the distance of a good ten feet from where she sat as I had opened the envelope.

"Some new inquiry case, perhaps?" she made a casual suggestion.

"Some previous business." I made the excuse and said nothing more.

We spent that last evening, before my departure for London, exploring the weapons at Old Lodge, that included twin flint-lock pistols that my aunt had first learned to shoot with. She seemed particularly fond of them.

The following morning, Mrs. Hutton, the caretaker's wife, provided me a carry-along luncheon and Mr. Hutton drove me to the village, where I was able to send off a response to Sir Avery to let him know that I was returning.

The trip back to London took several hours with connections made along the way. It was late in the evening when the train finally arrived at King's Cross station.

I would have preferred to meet with Sir Avery the following day with a chance to collect my thoughts and settle back in at the town house in Mayfair.

That was not to be, as my housekeeper, Mrs. Ryan, handed me a note that had been sent round by courier earlier that day and informed me that my presence was needed immediately upon my arrival.

"Something to eat first, miss?" Mrs. Ryan inquired as I put through a call for a cabman after letting the driver from the rail station depart.

I had no appetite. Instead, I quickly changed out of my travel costume as I waited for a new driver.

I retrieved my notebook from my writing desk and tucked it into my travel bag. I suddenly stopped as I came across the fountain pen Brodie had given me for my last birthday. It was elegant and undoubtedly quite expensive.

"Fer makin' yer notes," he had said.

I had cried, not because of what it was. I had other writing pens. Nor because it was so very expensive. It was because of what it meant, that he understood me, as few others had.

I put it in my bag as well. The cabman arrived shortly thereafter.

"When should I expect you, miss?" Mrs. Ryan asked as I seized my umbrella.

In truth, I had no idea. It was quite unusual for a meeting to be scheduled so late in the day. Yet, this was Sir Avery and the Special Services Agency. I told her not to wait supper as I left the town house.

On the ride to the Tower where the Agency had their offices, I thought again about that agreement I had made with Sir Avery, the very same agreement that had saved Brodie's life. I didn't regret it at the time.

However, I now wondered what it might mean, as Sir Avery seemed to call in that agreement I had made.

The offices of the Agency were under the Tower of London, in a rabbit-warren of ancient rooms and cells that had been converted for the purposes of secrecy.

The description was somewhat vague to say the least. The official version was that the Agency investigated and resolved delicate and at times dangerous threats against the Crown, the royal family, and others.

In the past, that had included conspiracies, counterfeit currency, and an assassination attempt against a member of the royal family, inquiry cases that Brodie and I had found ourselves involved in.

The unofficial version was that the *'situations'* the Agency dealt with were often of the utmost secrecy and never revealed on the crime pages of the daily newspapers.

I was signed in at the street entrance upon my arrival, then greeted by Alex Sinclair with some surprise on my part as it was quite late in the evening and he was often gone by that time.

We had first met on a previous case where he assisted with the breaking of a code that was critical to the inquiry case. Though he was quite young and not at all the stodgy sort, he was brilliant and always tinkering with some invention or another.

"I was asked to await your arrival and then immediately escort you to Sir Avery's office," he informed me.

"The telegram I received said that the matter was most urgent," I commented in an attempt to learn something of the matter as we wound through the maze of corridors and passageways toward Sir Avery's office.

He nodded as we continued down several steps and deeper below the main Tower.

"We have all be sworn to complete secrecy in the matter," he commented over his shoulder in a quiet tone.

"Not only would we lose our positions, but it was made clear there would be even more 'serious repercussions.' I haven't even spoken of it with Lucy."

Lucy Penworth was my very good friend who had once worked at the Times of London newspaper and more recently at the Agency. In addition, she and Alex were in a *'personal relationship.'*

She was intelligent, most observant, and I could only imagine how difficult it might be to keep one's work secret. And then there was Sir Avery.

He was from a titled family, a second son who had a distinguished military career, served in a handful of important posts, and was said to have acquired valuable experience and contacts abroad.

He had been chosen by the Queen to create a new and separate organization in the interest of protecting the Crown against clandestine threats. Hence, the Agency of Special Services.

We arrived at Sir Avery's office, a surprisingly stark set of rooms considering his status, family, and background. It was further insight into a man who was said by those who worked for him—Alex for one—that he had no time for extravagances. His priority was to 'get the job done,' as it were.

Alex knocked at the door. There was a brief pause, then a response. He did not continue with me into the office, but stepped aside at the opened door. We exchanged a brief look. His expression mirrored that urgent message received at Old Lodge. He then left.

Sir Avery rose from behind the desk and greeted me. "So good of you to respond to my telegram, Lady Forsythe."

As if it had been a social invitation instead of a summons. I would have pointed that out, however, the office door opened once more. Alex had returned.

"I beg your pardon, sir." He would have announced the arrival of the person with him.

However, no announcement was necessary as Brodie stepped past him, then abruptly halted as that dark gaze met mine.

"Now that you are both here..." Sir Avery announced, then informed Alex that he could leave with instructions to escort the other '*guest*' to the office as soon as he arrived.

Brodie was the first to recover, and equally surprised— actually angry might have better described his reaction.

"There seems to be a mistake..." he started to say.

Sir Avery cut him off. "No mistake. I have summoned you both here on a matter of grave importance. You are quite well recovered from your injuries, Mr. Brodie?"

"Aye, but there are matters ye may not be aware of. Miss Forsythe..."

There it was again, addressing me by my former name.

"She has only just returned after an extended time away and is not prepared to undertake any business on behalf of the Agency."

While I didn't care for the formality that he had used to mention me, I was somewhat in agreement with his excuse about my recent return to London.

Very well, I thought. Whatever Sir Avery had planned, I would simply decline.

"Sir Avery, I'm certain whatever the matter might be, Mr. Brodie is quite capable," I attempted to explain.

What matter might that be? More counterfeit currency? Something pinched during a recent parade to celebrate the Queen's birthday?

"Please be seated so that I may inform you of the matter at hand," Sir Avery replied, undaunted by anything that either Brodie or I had to say.

I took a chair across the desk from Sir Avery. Brodie chose

to remain standing, hands thrust into the pockets of his trousers, the expression on his face dark as thunder, as I had once heard someone described. It certainly was appropriate now.

The matter at hand, as Sir Avery went on to describe it, was the disappearance of an important member of the Queen's Privy Council.

"Sir Anthony Collingwood was last seen two days ago at Sandringham during a gathering of his Royal Highness's usual circle of gentlemen friends for a weekend of gaming.

"He is a close personal friend of the Prince of Wales as well as First Lord of the Admiralty, a position of grave importance. His disappearance is most unusual.

"There has been no word from him in the time since, and there are concerns for his welfare," he continued. "It is for that reason that I have summoned both of you to this office.

"You have demonstrated in the past an ability to make inquiries where others cannot, as well as success in previous inquiries, and that expertise is much needed at this time."

When Brodie would have again objected, Sir Avery simply ignored him and continued on.

"I have received very few details. However, we might be able to learn more when we are joined by his Royal Highness."

As if on cue in a stage performance, there was another knock at the door.

"He has insisted on meeting here rather than at the Palace or his London residence which might have raised undue attention," Sir Avery explained, and then stood to greet the Prince of Wales as he entered the office.

"I believe no introductions are necessary," he commented as Prince Edward Albert, known more familiarly to some as Bertie, took my hand and bowed over it. We had become less formally acquainted in a previous inquiry case that we had resolved for him.

"Lady Forsythe and I are well acquainted," he now greeted me. "You are quite well, it seems, after your recent travels which can be quite exhausting."

"Yes, quite well, Your Highness," I acknowledged with a quick glance over to where Brodie stood apart.

"No formalities, please," His Highness replied. "I believe we moved past that with our previous association." He nodded toward Brodie. "You do me a great favor now, sir, by making yourself available."

Brodie nodded in response. That '*previous association*' had been an assassination plot that Brodie and I had exposed and then thwarted. Afterward, we were thanked privately by him with the promise that if there was ever another need...

It seemed that there now was one.

"Lady Montgomery is well, I hope," he commented with the usual exchange of pleasantries.

I assured him that she was.

"Now that we are all present," Sir Avery interjected. "Please be seated. There is much to be discussed."

Three

～～

SIR ANTHONY COLLINGWOOD was from a well-placed family, highly educated, with a career in the military. He was now retired, as well as holding the very important position of First Lord of the Admiralty. And he was also a close personal friend of the Prince of Wales.

They had first met at Oxford. Afterward, Sir Anthony achieved a military career that the Prince would have preferred to possess himself; however it was rumored to have been vetoed by the Queen in the best interests of the Crown.

The friendship continued through the years. He was asked to join the Queen's private council upon his retirement from the British Navy, due to his exemplary achievements in the military that had included foreign service postings across the Empire.

Sir Anthony had recently accompanied His Highness on an extended tour of European and Asian countries, including India and Hong Kong, to acquaint him with the different cultures of the Empire, and he met regularly with the Queen's private council, advising on certain matters that pertained to the security of the Crown.

"I requested your presence at his behest," Sir Avery then explained, "for the reason that you both have experience in situations that have involved the Crown, and there is now a new and most serious situation that requires the utmost discretion and secrecy."

Particular discretion was necessary as we began our inquiries as the men present that weekend at Sandringham were well-placed, with more than one on the Queen's Council. In addition to hunting game, there had been other games with certain aspects that might be frowned upon were they made known.

As I listened to Sir Avery's account of the evening preceding Sir Anthony's disappearance, I conjured up all sorts of thoughts of what a gentleman's weekend would have included in addition to the usual round of hunting, gaming, and the other things men indulged in that might be frowned upon if it were made public.

"His Highness will be providing a list of those who were present."

"Quite so," the Prince of Wales replied and reached into the front of his long coat.

He handed the list to Sir Avery. "Some of the games were of a very...private nature, you understand," he explained with a look at me. "The sort of thing that men might indulge in along with the usual card games and some trivial gambling."

Sir Avery handed the list to Brodie. He glanced at it then handed it to me.

In the past I had glimpsed some of the *games* that men played at their private clubs. It was most...interesting and entertaining.

I had made the acquaintance of several of the men on that list socially at one time or another, and could only imagine what games took place at His Highness's country residence far from prying eyes, and wives. I forced my attention back to the situation at hand.

"Would it be possible to speak with the guests?" I inquired.

A look passed between Sir Avery and Prince Albert.

"In the interest of discretion, I have already spoken with most of the gentlemen who were there that night," Sir Avery replied. "None were aware of Sir Collingwood's disappearance. Do you have any questions, Mr. Brodie?"

He indicated the list in my hands.

"Was anything mentioned that might indicate some difficulty that evening between any of the gentlemen?" he asked.

"Wot, if any, ladies that might have been present as well? Is there a possibility that Sir Collingwood had a change of plans and might have returned early to London?"

A look passed between Sir Avery and the Prince of Wales.

"Bluntly spoken, Mr. Brodie," His Highness replied. "I assure you there was nothing to indicate any difficulty, and it is most certainly not in Sir Collingwood's nature to simply take himself off without letting others know. He is a man of discipline, principle, and integrity."

"Have inquiries been made at his office here in London?" I inquired.

"I sent my personal assistant to his offices to inquire, as I would usually after a sporting weekend," His Highness replied. "His staff have not seen him since his departure to join us."

"And the Admiralty offices as well?" I added.

"The same."

"What of his personal residence?" I asked.

"Not as yet," Sir Avery replied. "Under such unusual

circumstances there is obvious concern for his well-being, and due to his position as a member of the Queen's Privy Council. It is imperative that he is found safe as soon as possible."

"Please understand that Sir Collingwood is a friend of long-standing as well, and I am deeply concerned for him," the Prince of Wales added. "I am relying on your abilities now to find him."

"Of course," Brodie replied, but in a tone that was hardly pleased.

His Highness rose from his chair as he prepared to depart.

"You have been most discreet in the past, Lady Forsythe. I hope to have such circumspection now as well. Whatever you may need that I have not included in my previous conversation with Sir Avery, you have only to ask and it will be provided."

I thanked him.

Brodie waited until he had gone.

"A single person can easily make the necessary inquiries," he pointed out with obvious meaning. "There is no need for Miss Forsythe to be involved."

Sir Avery cut him off. "Lady Forsythe has the ability to make inquiries with certain parties due to her station, precisely as you have your own unique abilities, and His Highness specifically asked for her participation.

"You will undertake these inquiries together and hopefully all will be resolved quickly. It is not a *request*, Mr. Brodie."

"Sir...?" When he would have spoken again, he was immediately silenced.

"That is all, Mr. Brodie. Mr. Sinclair will provide you both with additional information that His Highness has made available. It is imperative that you begin without delay."

To say that Brodie was not pleased with the arrangement was quite obvious as we left Sir Avery's office, and there was no opportunity to discuss the matter as he continued some distance down the hallway. He waited until I caught up, and then we both entered Alex Sinclair's office.

Alex looked up with a frown, made all the more serious by those large glasses that gave him a very scholarly appearance. He brushed back the shock of dark hair that was forever falling over his forehead.

"Right." He came out of his chair. "So, it would seem that Sir Avery has explained the case at hand," he commented, coming round his desk to shake Brodie's hand. He gave me a smile.

"We have no information on Sir Collingwood's whereabouts after that last night at His Highness's country home at Sandringham. Point of fact, no one saw him leave. So, it would seem that is the place to start. Are you familiar with Sandringham?"

"I have been there on occasion, though it was some time ago," I replied.

I had accompanied my great-aunt to a holiday party she was invited to attend on behalf of the Princess of Wales after the latest construction of the manor was completed.

I didn't elaborate that it had included a weekend of shooting sports. My great-aunt had taken first prize, besting several of the men.

"That could be helpful" Alex commented. "Although," this was added with a look first at Brodie, then myself, "it is some distance from London. It may require an overnight stay.

"The servants have been instructed to make every accommodation. There is also an inn nearby the rail station," he added. "Sir Avery will want to know how soon you will be able to depart."

"There are arrangements that must be made," Brodie replied. "The morning train would seem best."

Arrangements? I did wonder if there was another case he was working? Or some other matter?

"Yes, of course," Alex replied. "I will see that your travel is arranged and meet you at the station. The train leaves St. Pancras at quarter past ten each day, and arrives in Sandringham, with the manor at Sandringham just beyond by coach."

He looked at me then at Brodie, as if anticipating some objection. There were several, however none that were mentioned.

"I will be at the rail station promptly tomorrow morning," I replied, then turned to leave.

"I'll make certain one of our drivers is available for you now," Alex replied, glancing from Brodie to me.

"That is not necessary," I informed them both.

"Not at all, Miss Forsythe." Once again there was that glance at Brodie then me. Alex picked up the mouthpiece to the device on his desk.

"Yes, right away," he confirmed. "A driver will be at the street entrance momentarily."

"Mr. Brodie?" he then inquired.

"No need for an extra driver. I will continue on after Miss Forsythe is delivered to Mayfair."

Delivered! Like a parcel, or coal for the coal bin!

"As I said, not necessary," I stiffly informed them both. "It's not so late at night that I cannot find a driver of my own."

"I do apologize, Miss Forsythe. You are far too valuable to the matter at hand. Sir Avery would insist of the Agency providing a driver for you as well," Alex replied.

At lease I was valuable to someone!

"Very well," I replied. "Is there anything else?"

"I will provide any additional information when we meet at the rail station in the morning."

The meeting with Alex concluded, I spun about and headed for the entrance at the street at the same time I fought to bring my thoughts and emotions back under control.

I suppose I should have known that Brodie might be there as well, but I had foolishly not considered that. The telegram I had received at Old Lodge said nothing about it and I was not prepared for it.

And in that brief exchange, I had sensed the anger that was still there. Except for the one brief comment that necessary inquiries could easily be made by one person—himself, there had been little if any recognition that I was even in the room!

What did you expect after the way you took yourself off with just that brief note? That little inner voice that had the way of speaking up at the most inopportune moments intruded once again.

And now?

I really did need to speak with Templeton about the subject of muses and interfering spirits. There had to be a way to quiet that bloody nagging little voice that wasn't at all helpful at the moment.

I navigated the hallways, made a wrong turn, and ended up in that part of the Tower that was in fact a prison, in front of one of those ancient cells where others had been imprisoned down through the centuries.

For the writer in me it was an unwelcome metaphor of the present situation. I doubled back to the passage and quickened my pace.

Trying to escape, are you?

"Stuff it!" I replied. Yet, that thought returned...What *had* I expected?

I knew Brodie quite well with that typical Scots demeanor, the stubbornness, his temper in certain situations, that he had also accused me of.

And then there was that stinging comment during our last case, that things had changed, that he didn't want me to be part of?

What the devil was that about? It was something I had thought of countless times during our time apart. Did he regret the marriage?

The toe of my boot caught at the edge of a raised stone in the passage, and I silently cursed again. Let that inner voice deal with that, I thought!

"Mikaela...!"

It was then that I felt Brodie's hand on my elbow, steadying me.

"Are ye all right?"

A simple question and the immediate thought came—No, I was not all right! I had been caught completely unprepared for this meeting, unprepared for him.

And now?

A driver had not yet arrived and I considered simply leaving, not at all certain at the moment that I wanted to be near Brodie. However, the guard politely asked us to wait inside that fortified, heavily gated entrance.

I couldn't help wondering how many prisoners, both royal and otherwise over the centuries, had awaited their fate at this precise location. It was quite ironic.

Brodie thanked the warder as we continued to wait, the silence between us almost like a voice shouting at me. He was too close as that familiar scent of cinnamon that was always about him drifted over me.

Bloody damn Scot!

We stood there like two strangers, the warder going about his duties as he signed in an envelope from a courier, received a telephone call that filled the heavy silence, then went to deliver that envelope.

"Ye have been well?" Brodie inquired.

"Yes, and yourself?" I replied, cordial as well, as I shifted my bag to my other hand.

I had thought a dozen times how we would meet after I returned, things that needed to be said. I wasn't fool enough to think that he might not be angry. But this? That polite coolness, almost indifference, after our work, after...everything else?

"Yer travels were agreeable?" he then inquired.

Agreeable? And that question, polite, grated like fingernails across a chalkboard, as if it was a trip for health, rather than to get away from that last argument, his overbearing attitude, and that parting comment that he didn't want me to be part of this any longer.

Our inquiry cases? The marriage? Did he now consider it a mistake?

I refused to be drawn into an argument here.

"My aunt and Lily were quite taken with Africa," I replied instead.

"No wild creatures brought back to Sussex Square?" he commented.

"Not at all," I replied.

"And Lily is well?"

"Quite well and now back at her lessons, much to her disappointment that now includes a young woman to teach her, help her with manners and deportment."

Awkwardness drew out between us and I silently cursed the continued wait.

"How is young Rory?" I then inquired, since it had been

considerable time since I had seen him, and I did know that Brodie felt a deep responsibility for him.

"He is quite well, thank ye for askin'."

And that, without actually saying so, was obviously all he was going to say. I tried a different topic.

"Have you taken new inquiry cases?" I asked, as I would have anyone I had met after a long absence.

"Two cases, both quickly resolved to the satisfaction of the clients."

Two cases. He had simply continued on in the time I was away. I pushed back irritation and was grateful when the warder returned and announced that a driver had arrived.

Brodie thanked him and escorted me to the street. He gave the driver the address of the town house in Mayfair.

I ignored his offer of assistance, hiked my skirt, and climbed into the coach.

What did you expect?

I frowned as I settled onto the seat at one end of the coach.

You sent round that note with no other explanation and then left for four months.

Five months, I thought. Five very long and boring months.

You were the one who took yourself off to Africa, a place you had already been...

"Oh, do be quiet!" It was only when I caught the sudden frown on Brodie's face, as he settled onto the seat across, that I realized I had spoken aloud. And I thought the evening couldn't get any worse!

The rest of the ride to Mayfair passed quietly. Too quietly.

When we arrived, I hastily made for the door of the coach in order to make a quick departure, and was abruptly brought up short. My skirt was caught in the door opening.

Oh, bloody hell! I thought as I attempted to free myself, one foot on the curb, the other on the step of the coach.

"Ye seem to be caught," Brodie commented.

Did I detect a trace of humor in that?

"Thank you so much," I sarcastically replied.

As I was soundly caught, my choices were obvious— attempt to carefully dislodge my skirt from the opening, simply tear the blasted thing free, or...

"Ye need to be more careful."

How very useful, I thought, as I gave him a look that usually would have stopped a gentleman in his tracks. This was Brodie, however, who never made any claim to be one.

He exited the coach at the opposite side, circled round, then took hold of my skirt and freed it quite handily from the opening all the while the driver attempted to ignore both of us.

There was a moment as we stood there, the hem of my skirt in his hand, myself wishing for something appropriate to say.

I looked at him then—that dark gaze, that bloody handsome face with that dark beard and that slash of a scar that made him seem even...more so!

"Sir?" the driver reminded from atop the coach. "Will you be continuing on, sir?"

Brodie released the hem of my skirt. "Good evening, Miss Forsythe." He then called out to the driver before climbing back inside the coach.

"Number 204 at the Strand."

I swore I would not look back at that departing coach as I climbed the steps to the front entrance of the town house.

Liar...

I was relieved that my housekeeper was not at the door to inquire about the evening, or the meeting at the Agency, or

Brodie once again as she had several times since my return from my aunt's safari travels.

It was quite late. I went up to my room, undressed, and promptly lay awake for the next several hours.

I finally gave up, rose, and went back down to the front parlor where I kept my writing desk.

I spent the next few hours making notes regarding Sir Collingwood's disappearance.

Brodie and I were to make the usual inquiries, yet after that meeting at the Tower it could hardly be said that we were working together.

For once that nagging little voice was silent.

My housekeeper, Mrs. Ryan, eventually appeared with coffee and warm biscuits. I informed her that I would be leaving soon with no certainty when I would be returning. I caught the arch of her eyebrows.

"And Mr. Brodie?" she inquired.

"He has a new case. His return is uncertain as well." I left it with that simple explanation, the less said the better.

When I had dressed and packed my carpet bag, I telephoned for a driver to take me to the rail station.

I then placed a call to Sussex Square and learned that my great-aunt and Lily had returned as well, by motor car for part of the distance. I cringed at the thought.

"Mr. Stewart was most accommodating and making a trip to Edinburgh as well," she explained.

The motor car was a fairly recent acquisition, and she was absolutely fascinated by it. However, the roadways in Scotland, no more than coach roads, were quite dangerous.

It did seem that caution had prevailed, and she and Lily had caught the train in Edinburgh to London.

"The weather had begun to set in quite thick at Old Lodge,

and Mr. Hutton suggested we return or we might be there for weeks. And I do need to meet with your sister about wedding plans. I do hope you will be available as well."

Of course. I did, however, let her know that I would be gone for a few days.

"Hmmm, yes, Sandringham is it?" she commented over the telephone. "I had heard that His Highness had returned somewhat abruptly from his usual stay with friends."

Why, I thought, was I surprised that she was so well informed, most particularly where the royal family was concerned? And in spite of Sir Avery's insistence on absolute secrecy from everyone involved.

"Most interesting," she continued, then added, "Lily and I will be quite well occupied until your return. With Mr. Munro's guidance, I will be contacting Mr. Thurkle regarding a new sword I am thinking of acquiring for Lily. She must have her own for protection for whenever she is out and about."

Edward Turkle, sword-maker of the finest military blades.

"Do let us know when you have returned, dear."

Thank heavens for Mr. Munro, I thought. My great-aunt and Lily were in safe hands.

With arrangements made, I departed for St. Pancras rail station when the driver arrived.

Four

I TOLD myself that it mattered not if Brodie wasn't there.

If not, if some matter had delayed him—a new inquiry case perhaps, then I would simply carry on to Sandringham on my own.

All very well and good. I should have known better.

He was there with that usual diligence from having served with the MET, accompanied by Alex Sinclair who had brought final instructions from Sir Avery as he handed us our travel tickets.

"There is a telegraph office at the rail station at Wolferton which is very near Sandringham if you should need to make contact with the Agency." He looked from me to Brodie, then continued.

"The staff at Sandringham have been made aware of your arrival and that you are to be given every courtesy, as well as access to all areas. If you should need to remain for an extended period of time, you will be provided accommodations."

Remain? I had not anticipated that. It was my intention to complete our inquiries quickly.

What did you expect? That inner voice piped in.

"That should cover everything," Alex concluded. "Again, Sir Avery has requested that you are to remain in contact with any progress," he added as the last call went out for us to board.

"Do either of you have any questions?"

"That will do," Brodie responded, the first words he had spoken since my arrival, as I walked to the railcar where we were to board.

We had been provided accommodations in a compartment rather than seats in the main carriage, although that would have been preferable as it would have eliminated the necessity for any conversation.

Perhaps a window seat, I thought now, where I could simply ignore him.

That hope was dashed as other passengers, an older man and woman, had already arrived and had taken window seats across from each other.

"We most certainly have a pleasant day for our trip," the woman commented with a smile.

That depended on one's definition of pleasant, I thought. Brodie seemed to be of the same opinion as he removed his hat, his expression appearing quite doomed. That was the only word for it. I was in agreement.

"It was dreadful when we first arrived a week ago," our companion prattled on. "It rained the entire time. We have been to theater several times though. Most enjoyable."

That of course required my part of the conversation. I politely inquired which play they had seen.

"As You Like It," she replied. "And only in London for a brief engagement. We are celebrating our anniversary and were fortunate to obtain tickets."

And that required the next obvious question as I took my

seat at the other end of the compartment near the door by the outside passageway, and Brodie took the one across.

"We've been married thirty-five years." She glowed in response. "Three daughters and two sons."

Thirty-five years? Good heavens! Brodie and I hadn't been able to manage one year and some months.

"Ye are to be congratulated," he commented.

"May I ask, how long you have been married?" the woman inquired, making the natural assumption as we were traveling together, and I was still wearing the bronze wedding band Brodie had given me.

That dark gaze met mine. I started to reply something vague that wouldn't bring about more questions. Under the circumstances, I had no desire to be drawn into a conversation about the merits of marriage.

"I apologize. You must forgive my wife's curiosity."

"We've been married a few months," Brodie finally provided.

"You are quite recently married then," our companion chirped. "How delightful."

Delightful? I ignored the look Brodie gave me from across the compartment.

"You are just beginning your lives together, a very exciting time," she continued. "I do hope that you will celebrate many happy years together."

At present that seemed highly unlikely.

I didn't reply. It wasn't necessary, the woman was capable of carrying on a full conversation on her own.

"My dear husband, I am certain, would tell you that patience and understanding are the key to a happy marriage. And the ability to admit when one is wrong." She aimed a look at her husband with that last remark.

Patience? Understanding? Admitting one was wrong? Oh, my.

Her husband was very definitely not a Scot.

Our companion's husband gently reminded his wife that we might perhaps have other matters to concern us on the journey.

"That is my husband's way of suggesting that I have spoken out of turn. I hope that I have not offended," she chirped, much like a little bird.

With a long look at me, Brodie assured her that she had not. And it was not necessary for us to join the conversation even if we had wanted.

Our companion was most capable as she commented on the countryside once we had left London property behind, an overlong description of the play they had seen, and then about their children.

Chirp, chirp, chirp.

We arrived at Wolferton station in Norfolk just after midday and then continued on to Sandringham by coach.

The manor had originally been purchased by Prince Albert several years prior, intended for the young Prince of Wales when he had his own family.

Over the years it had been torn down, rebuilt, and the surrounding property transformed to accommodate the Prince of Wales's growing family and his love of country sports that included hunting and other 'games.'

It provided a respite from duties in the city, and he often departed Marlborough House for Sandringham, met there by close friends, while the Princess chose to remain in London.

It was an arrangement that seemed to suit both of them. She then joined him with their growing family for holidays and long stays in the countryside. The fact that his hunting excursions in the country were rumored to include his mistress of the moment was apparently tolerated by the Princess.

That brought us to the previous several days, when the Prince of Wales had been entertaining that close circle of friends once more, and Sir Anthony Collingwood had disappeared.

Sandringham was like a grand lady, with double wings of Jacobean architecture in red brick, with an elaborate conservatory off the main entrance, and vast gardens spread around.

It was said to have over thirty bedrooms, a formal dining hall, as well as a ballroom, a second dining room for smaller parties, and a grand hall for family holiday celebrations. There were also living quarters for over two hundred servants and staff, many who had lived in and about Sandringham village all their lives.

The ride from the rail station had been mostly a silent one. That changed as soon as the grand estate came into view. It was monstrous, with two stories and spread out amid gardens that rivaled that of Buckingham Palace. So much for a *simple country home,* as it had been described.

"How the bloody hell are we to search for clues to the man's disappearance?" Brodie commented with a dark glower out the coach window. "It would take the full staff of the Metropolitan Police,"

I was of much the same opinion.

Even so, Alex Sinclair had informed us before we departed that billiards and other gaming that the prince's guests had enjoyed during that recent stay usually took place in the conservatory. That seemed a place to begin.

"We'll be fortunate not to get lost in the bloody place."

The sarcasm was there. I chose to ignore it.

"I'm certain we will be escorted by one of the servants. According to Sir Avery, they have been given instructions to assist us in whatever manner we might need."

The master of the household appeared as we arrived at the entrance and introduced himself. Mr. Compton announced that he had been in contact with the Prince of Wales and he had been instructed that we were to be provided every courtesy during our '*visit*,' including accommodations for the night if our stay extended.

He was dressed in a simply cut suit of clothes rather than royal livery that would have been required in London.

Brodie assured him that we would prefer to take up our responsibilities immediately so not to inconvenience anyone.

Mr. Compton nodded. "Everything has been left as it was two days ago. I will show you to the conservatory."

The entrance hall was connected to what was referred to as the saloon. From there, we were escorted down a hallway that contained a rich carpet over wood floors, and walls crowded with portraits of what I could only assume were long-dead ancestors or other persons of note.

As we reached the end of the hallway, Mr. Compton announced the other servants had been instructed that we were not to be disturbed.

I caught the faint sniff of disapproval as well as the curious glances of a handful of other servants at an adjacent hallway as we then followed him into the red brick conservatory with arched floor-to-ceiling windows that looked out on the gardens.

Another servant waited just inside the entrance. We were informed that Mr. Flannery, head steward, had attended the

Prince of Wales and guests during their stay and when it was discovered that Sir Collingwood had gone missing.

Mr. Flannery was older, in much the same attire as Mr. Compton.

"He has been instructed to assist in whatever way you might need in the matter, and should be able to answer any questions you have about the evening in question.

"You have only to let him know if I may be of further service," Mr. Compton added, then stiffly bowed and departed.

Brodie thanked Mr. Flannery and told him that we would let him know if we had any questions.

"Of course, sir."

"Do they give instruction to servants in how to be difficult and condescending?" Brodie said in a lowered voice as we proceeded inside the conservatory.

More than a half dozen words? And condescending? I smiled to myself.

If he wasn't careful, we might have a full-blown conversation, I thought, and simply answered, "Of course. However, some are born to it."

There was another muttered comment which was obviously in Gaelic.

"Ye canna mean they have that way already about them while still in their nappies?"

I left him with that as I continued along the length of the large gaming table with chairs set about in the center of the room. Smaller tables sat along the two long sides of the conservatory.

One of those was set with a chess board and pieces, another set with a cribbage board, with yet another set with dice and a leather cup.

We each continued down the long sides of the building with those tall windows with palm trees set between.

I made a sketch of the large room, that included the entrance, a set of exit doors at the far end of the conservatory, as well as a barely noticeable side door set into wood panels that lined the wall opposite those windows.

I then sketched the gaming tables, including the large center table where cards still remained, as well as the billiards table toward the far end.

It was now quite bare of cue sticks and gaming balls that had obviously been returned to the cabinet nearby. So much for everything left as it was that last night.

Chairs about the center table were positioned as they might have been the last night, and it appeared that baccarat had been the game of choice.

The *gaming shoe* was there, along with cards for what might have been the final game of the night, some turned over, others not, but with a set of cards displayed before the shoe— the obvious winning hand.

"Are ye are familiar with the game?" Brodie asked.

I did know a little about it, learned on one of my travels.

"It's a game of strategy. One bets on the bank or the player who possesses the shoe."

"A gentleman's game," he commented. "Ye have played it as well?"

"I was a guest of one of the players on one of my travels abroad."

He then moved around the table where the cards had been left just as they had been played that last game.

When he didn't reply, I continued to explain what I thought might be useful.

"I was curious about the game, and one of the players who was in our travel party was kind enough to explain it to me.

"There could be something the cards might tell us," I added. "It is possible that there might have been some disagreement over a winning draw that might have sent Sir Collingwood off," I suggested.

He didn't look up as he continued to observe the table. "A substantial bet that was lost?"

"It has happened," I stated. "The object of the game is to bet which hand will have the greatest value with the highest score of cards up to a total of nine," I continued, since I was the only one carrying on this conversation.

"Aye."

"The tens and face cards are all counted as zero. The Ace is worth one, the two is worth two, and other cards accordingly with the goal of getting as close as possible to a winning draw of nine.

"Bets are placed, then made on the highest count among the players and have been known to be made with jewelry, a prize racehorse, or..."

"A woman?" he suggested.

It was a possibility, I thought, considering His Highness's history with mistresses and other *arrangements for entertainment* that were quite well-known. And perhaps someone whose name was not on that list His Highness had provided.

"A lady with a penchant for cigarettes, it would seem." He picked up the remnant of one from a silver dish on the game table.

"The dark foreign kind. And one who prefers the color red." He handed the stained cigarette butt to me.

"So, it would seem," I replied.

It was most certainly possible that His Highness's guests

had included the current woman he favored. Or was it someone else with the unusual but not entirely unique habit of smoking a cigarette? Entertainment for the guests?

I handed the cigarette back to him, then made a note of it in my notebook. Brodie removed an envelope from his inside jacket pocket and tucked the cigarette inside.

Conversation continued to be limited to our observations, much as it was in the beginning of our partnership.

So be it, I thought. But there was something else along with it, something in those few words we exchanged, and his comments.

I wanted very much to speak with him about it, however it was very obvious by his responses that he did not wish to speak with me other than our observations about Sir Collingwood's disappearance.

So here we were, quite literally ordered to work together in this new inquiry. But the word *together*, somewhat of a misnomer.

I could have refused Sir Avery's summons, and perhaps should have. Brodie's coolness, almost indifference, was aggravating and painful.

However, Sir Avery had been most adamant. I had tried to explain it to Brodie before I left with Lily and my great-aunt for Africa months earlier. But he refused to listen. And now?

Men could be so obstinate, most particularly a Scot. They seemed to pride themselves on it.

I had experienced that before as well, but this was different, and I couldn't help a twinge of uncertainty when I had always been most certain and in control of my emotions.

I continued to make my own observations, writing them in my notebook as I passed the other tables in the conservatory.

As I examined that chess game further, it was apparent that

it had been well underway with several pieces captured by both players, while at another table dice had been the game of choice. At yet another table, a game of cribbage had taken place.

A silver salver sat at yet another small table with two chairs. It contained the remnants of a dark liquid that caught my attention. The contents were thick and smelled slightly sweet.

Brodie stopped me when I would have tasted it in an attempt to try to identify it. "Ye dinna want to do that. It's opium," he explained. "It's been cooked down from seeds and quite potent."

I was well aware of the presence of the drug in certain circles, particularly among the lower classes in the East End. And there were the usual rumors, of course, about it's being found in some of those exclusive London men's clubs.

From my experience during our inquiry cases, I knew that it was usually smoked in a pipe. Or in rare cases consumed as a pill, according to our friend Mr. Brimley, the chemist, those pills often prescribed for ladies with nervous complaints.

Opium had been banned some years before, yet that didn't seem to end the availability or the demand. According to something Brodie had once said, smugglers simply found another way to bring it into the country out from under the eye of the authorities.

I returned the salver to the table, then made a note about the discovery.

"It seems that His Highness or at least some of his guests indulge," I commented.

A gentleman's gathering in the country for gambling, apparently at least one woman who was present, and other *entertainments,* including illegal drugs.

Most interesting, but what did that tell us about Sir Collingwood's disappearance?

We continued our separate inspections around the conservatory. The Prince had assured that everything was left the way it was that last night before it was discovered that Sir Anthony had disappeared and the other guests had departed.

Still, it was obvious that the servants, or someone, had straightened the room and I wondered what might have been removed.

All in the interest of protecting the reputation of those present? Or perhaps one particular person—the Prince of Wales?

I might have missed the telltale gleam if the late afternoon sunlight was not slanted just so through one of those arched windows: something on the floor between two chairs at the table. I pulled back one of the chairs and knelt to retrieve the item.

"What have ye found?" Brodie asked.

It glittered in my hand, something the servants had apparently overlooked.

"Red lip-coloring, a fondness for Turkish cigarettes, and," I held aloft the piece of jewelry. "A gold chain with a pendant."

It seemed that the woman in question had expensive tastes. The pendant held a large stone. I handed it to Brodie.

"It does appear to be real gold," he announced as he examined it. "Perhaps a gift from one of the gentlemen."

"A special friend to one of the gentlemen? Or possibly payment for a night of companionship?"

"Aye, perhaps."

The mistress of His Highness? Or did it belong to someone else? I added the question to the growing list.

"It could be useful," he commented, and tucked the necklace into the envelope along with that cigarette.

We spent the next couple of hours retracing our steps to make certain we hadn't missed anything in the conservatory.

Mr. Flannery had returned to inquire if we wanted to see any other rooms during our visit.

Brodie inquired about Sir Collingwood's private rooms for his stay that weekend.

"Of course, sir."

The door in that one wall that I had made note of when we first arrived opened onto a hallway into the main palace, with another door directly across.

"And this room?" Brodie inquired.

"That is a bathing chamber, sir." Mr. Flannery replied.

A bathing chamber on the main floor, just outside the gaming room.

How very interesting, I thought.

"Would you care to see it, sir?"

Brodie nodded.

"Perhaps yourself and not the lady," Mr. Flannery suggested.

I stepped past him, opened the door and entered the room.

It was elaborately decorated and included a chaise, a clawfoot tub, and a curious attached fixture mounted overhead at the end of a pipe.

Where a man, or woman, or possibly both might refresh themselves afterward? Or perhaps there was some other intended use...?

Two towels lay on the floor where they had obviously been discarded. It did appear two persons had been the last occupants. I glanced over at Brodie. He frowned as he made notice of it as well.

"I must remind the housemaids to clean the rooms once you have concluded your inspection," Mr. Flannery commented with that same stoic expression.

Brodie looked over at me. "Make yer notes and then we'll continue on."

Notes were one thing, however, I did wonder how to describe the overhead fixture.

When making inquiries in a case where a crime has been committed, I had discovered over almost two years, there were often gruesome discoveries. Then, there were the 'private habits' of those we encountered.

In addition to the well-known rumors about His Highness's habits, it did seem as if his guests had indulged in some additional '*recreation*' during their stay last weekend.

There was that particular fixture mounted over the bathtub, along with an assortment of jars and bottles. Then there was a length of rope that appeared to be made of satin. There was also what appeared to be several rolled pieces of wool that had been discarded into a basket. I was somewhat familiar with them from the earliest part of my more private relationship with Brodie.

I made several notes as he asked, "Might we see Sir Collingwood's private room now?"

"Of course, sir," Mr. Flannery replied without the slightest change of expression or reaction at what we had discovered in the bathroom.

We followed Mr. Flannery to a lift at the end of the hallway beyond that bathing chamber, and discreetly hidden behind carved wood double doors.

"The rooms Sir Collingwood usually occupies, along with other guests, are some distance apart on the second floor."

After arriving at the second floor, he accompanied us to

that suite of rooms, and opened the door onto the main sitting room.

"If there is anything else, sir...?" Mr. Flannery started to say.

Brodie immediately thanked him. "That will be all."

He nodded and left us to our observations as I slowly walked about the room. Its thick window coverings were drawn this late in the day, the chamber lit by several electric fixtures.

It was said that His Highness had the latest amenities installed for when his family visited Sandringham. And obviously for 'guests' as well.

Water was provided to each room through a series of pipes with running water from a water tower on the grounds of the estate. Electricity was provided by a gas-powered plant.

The formal parlor for the suite was decorated as one might expect of a hunting lodge, with the heads of a water buffalo, a lion, deer, and boar that ran along the tastes of my father, and which I always thought quite garish.

The parlor provided no additional clues and we continued into the adjoining bedchamber.

"It does seem that either Sir Collingwood is an extremely tidy person, or the rooms have been cleaned and quite thoroughly," Brodie commented.

I was of much the same opinion as I moved about the room, looking for anything out of the ordinary that might tell us something about his stay and that last night before Sir Collingwood disappeared.

Yet, in spite of everything in its place, there did seem to be a strange fragrance in the room that had obviously been closed off the past few days. It wasn't a woman's fragrance but something else.

"Juniper," I remarked as it came to me at last.

Brodie looked over at me. "I beg yer pardon? Have ye found something?"

"There is the scent of juniper in the room. I recognize it from the forest around Old Lodge."

I caught the change of expression on his face when I mentioned Old Lodge, a place that held memories for us both. He frowned but said nothing as he continued to inspect the wardrobe and a table set with a decanter with what might have been brandy and two crystal tumblers.

I continued my own search and discovered the source of that familiar scent.

"It is here," I announced as I found a crushed spring of juniper caught in the double doors that led out onto a balcony.

Brodie followed me out onto the balcony.

The brisk air was refreshing after the mustiness of the room, with steps that led down to the gardens below. Brodie immediately followed those steps and disappeared into the growing darkness.

I eventually caught the glow from the beam of the hand-held light he always carried. He returned with a thoughtful expression.

"It appears that Sir Collingwood may have taken a late-night walk about the grounds, however there are no juniper trees nearby. There are footprints but not enough light to see beyond the garden."

"The forest where His Highness and guests usually hunt is just beyond the gardens," I replied.

He nodded. "And not enough light about to tell us where those prints may lead. We will need to return tomorrow."

It was obvious by the disappointment in his voice that he had hoped we might be able to conclude our search for clues into Sir Collingwood's disappearance and return to London the same day. I had hoped for the same. However, that was not to be.

I tucked the piece of juniper into my bag and we returned to the bedchamber to continue our search for anything else that might tell us something about that last night.

The bed linens had been changed, discovered when Brodie pulled back the brocade comforter and ran his hands over the surface of the linens, while I searched the adjoining bathroom.

Unlike the one off the conservatory, there was nothing unusual there. A linen towel had been dropped into a basket for staff to collect. If the lady in question had been in these rooms there was nothing to indicate it.

I returned to the main bedchamber and continued my inspection at the writing desk where a man of Sir Collingwood's expertise and habit might make notes. Everything there was in order as well—parchment stationery and pen with a blotter to prevent the ink smearing. All of it apparently untouched.

Brodie had returned to the small parlor.

"The hearth is clean as well," he commented. "It would seem that Sir Collingwood did not have a fire that last night. Or possibly it has been cleaned. We need to speak with the servants who were present."

We had been informed by Sir Avery that the servants had all been questioned about anything unusual they might have seen or heard that last night of the gentlemen's get-together.

Mr. Flannery reminded us of that.

"Nevertheless, sir," Brodie told him. "We wish to speak with the servants who were on this floor that last night."

There were four servants who had been assigned to the floor the night Sir Collingwood disappeared, to see to various duties should he or any of the other guests require anything—a late supper, perhaps additional drink, a book from the library, more coal for the fire, or a late-night tonic against some discomfort.

We met with each of the servants in the ground floor library. They appeared one-by-one, escorted by Mr. Compton who then hovered silently nearby.

We spoke first with the floor steward, who assured us there was nothing amiss that last night. Sir Collingwood had retired for the evening just after midnight and there had been no further exchange with him.

The footman confirmed that same information. He had made certain there was enough coal in the coal bin that night as the temperatures had grown quite chilly with the changing season.

Monsieur Duladier, the valet who attended Sir Colling-wood that night, saw to it that his clothes were cleaned and pressed for the evening and other entertainments, then returned late in the evening to make certain that all was in readiness for Sir Collingwood to retire for the night.

There was some difficulty between the man's obvious French accent and Brodie's thick Scots accent.

Although whether the difficulty was merely one of language or perhaps contrived on Monsieur Duladier's part, I repeated the questions in French much to his surprise.

Had there been any late arrivals for the weekend that were not on the list provided? I asked. He replied in surprisingly excellent English that had not been so clear earlier.

Had there been any messages or telegrams delivered or received? There had not been.

Was there any indication that Sir Collingwood might have left his chambers at any time after he retired for the evening?

"No, madame," Duladier replied. "He did not leave his chambers."

Yet, those footprints Brodie had found below Sir Collingwood's chambers told something different.

"Might he have had a visitor late at night?"

His response was the same.

"Will that be all, madame?" the valet then inquired.

I was quite done with the man, with no patience for rudeness or condescending attitudes.

It was Brodie who informed him, "That will be all."

It did seem that our inquiries were at an end, to be taken up again in the morning when there was sufficient daylight to investigate those footprints Brodie had discovered at the base of the steps.

"May we see to your accommodations now, sir?" Mr. Flannery inquired.

"Thank ye kindly, but no. We will be staying in the village and returning in the morning," Brodie informed him.

I looked at him with some surprise, however staying over in the village for the night would give us the opportunity to discuss what we had learned, away from walls that had ears.

"You will require a coach then, sir," Mr. Flannery replied. "I will have Mr. Compton inform the stablemaster."

It was late in the evening when we finally arrived at the village. Brodie had the driver take us to the only inn in the small community.

"Yer in luck," the woman at the counter told us. "I have one room left, wot with those who are here for the races."

Brodie frowned. "That will do."

The woman was the chatty sort and continued as people do who lived in places beyond London and were often quite friendly.

"We thought His Highness might have one of his horses entered in the races," she continued. "But I was told he has returned early to London." She turned the guest book around for Brodie to sign.

"He's quite a fan as well and usually has one of his horses entered. He's a beauty...the horse, I mean.

"Breakfast is served beginning at seven in the morning on race days," she continued as she handed Brodie the room key. "And there is still supper available, if ye've a mind to. Me girl, Molly, can fix ye up with some stewed chicken fresh today."

Neither of us had eaten since before leaving London. Brodie nodded and our hostess directed us to the common room.

I have been in taverns before and this one was much the same. They all seemed to have the same things in common, no matter the part of England—patrons at the long bar with others at several small tables, and boisterous conversation, a game or two of dice in progress.

However, instead of gossip or shouts among dock workers and other laborers as I had heard in London, the conversations here in the Norfolk countryside were about the forthcoming races, with side bets being made over conversation about the owner, the jockey, or a particular horse.

Most of the patrons were at the bar where a lively discussion was underway about a local horse as Brodie found an empty table. The discussion was soon joined by two other patrons who argued that the animal was a slow starter and not a 'mudder,' with the weather that was expected the following day.

"It seems that we should get an early start in the morning," I commented, so to avoid those who were attending the races.

He nodded, then went to the bar to inquire about supper while I took out my notebook.

I had just set pen to the page when the table was suddenly jarred, creating a vivid streak of ink across the page.

"My, but ain't you a pretty one."

I looked into the bleary-eyed gaze of a stout older man with ruddy cheeks and somewhat patchwork gray beard. He was dressed like the patrons in a worn jacket and trousers, and leaned toward me in a haze of beer, hands braced on the edge of the table.

"We don't see yer sort around here exceptin' when His Highness is about and one of his guests drop by."

"Perhaps recently with a woman?"

I thought it worth asking since we now knew there had been a woman among the guests at Sandringham.

He shook his head and I thought the exertion of that might send him toppling over, he was so wobbly. However, he recovered sufficiently and steadied himself by bracing his hands on the table.

"No women other than servants, and I would know as I keep the stables near the station. The gentlemen guests all came in together and there wasn't a woman among 'em unless she was dressed the same as themselves." He laughed at that.

"Yer the first in a long while and a pretty one. How about I buy you a pint?"

I politely refused.

"Too high and mighty for Darby, are you?"

"Not at all..." I started to explain to him that I was there with someone even as that person returned.

"The lady said she didna care to take a drink with ye. Move along."

54

Brodie had returned and, more or less politely, asked him to leave.

"Ye will leave now, and not bother the lady again."

"The lady might have a different answer." Darby replied, weaving slightly as he confronted Brodie who was several inches taller and not the slightest impaired.

"What gives you the right?"

"The lady is my wife!" Brodie responded in a tone that left no doubt or room for argument.

All things considered I was as surprised as Mr. Darby. Since our that first meeting the day before after my return to London, he had been remote, almost indifferent, refusing to engage in anything more than professional conversation necessary to the case.

"Wife?" Mr. Darby replied in a somewhat drunken slur. Then he laughed.

"No bother," he said then with hands raised. "But a lucky man, you be with such a fair one."

He chuckled and then left, bracing himself against another table as he made his way back to the bar.

Brodie watched him leave, then took the chair opposite at the table. That dark gaze met mine, briefly.

"The girl will bring supper."

And that was the total of our supper conversation. Afterward, we climbed the stairs to the second floor over the tavern.

We found the room and Brodie inserted the large iron key into the lock.

The room was small but clean, with what passed for an overstuffed chair, a small table, wash stand, and a narrow bed against the far wall that was hardly meant for two people.

"I'll stay in the common room below," he commented with a look at the bed.

"That's not necessary..."

It certainly had never been an issue in the past when we were working together or...when not working together. The bed in the adjacent room at the office on the Strand was hardly larger.

But this was different. And I had to admit I felt a tightness deep inside that made it hard to breathe with this difficulty between us.

"You will hardly be able to get any sleep with the tavern full of customers," I pointed out. "Heaven knows if any of them will go home for the night."

"Mikaela..."

I heard something in his voice. He hesitated, then finally agreed.

"I'll take the chair."

So, there we were, in a tavern in Norfolk, with that narrow bed and an overstuffed chair, which the description defied as there appeared to be little stuffing in it.

I had not seriously considered that we might need to stay over. However, it was not the first time and I undressed down to my chemise and petticoat then crawled under the blankets.

I wakened sometime later to the sounds of Brodie shifting about in the chair, followed by silence.

I had given him a blanket from the bed earlier, however there was no coal stove and the room had grown quite cold through the night. I removed a blanket from the bed, the table and that chair dark shadows, as I crossed the room.

I was careful not to waken him if he should have gone back to sleep as I laid the second blanket over him. He had not, that dark gaze meeting mine in the half-light that spilled through the window.

I saw so many things there. Memories perhaps from the

past when we had shared a room? And a bed? Or perhaps only weariness from tossing about in an attempt to get comfortable?

I wanted very much to ease whatever it was I saw there—questions, words left unspoken? Anger? Was it still there?

Then, I felt the brush of his hand on mine.

The things I thought I saw were still there in that dark gaze, along with something else. Something that might have been sadness? Or regret?

Whatever it was, I felt it as well.

"*Caileag,*" that Scots accent wrapped around the word.

I had no way of knowing what it meant, my Gaelic limited to a few words and phrases. But there was something in the way he said it, a softness what wrapped around it, far different from the anger that had sent me from him months before.

Then his hand slipped from mine.

I returned to the bed, and lay there in the darkness unable to sleep.

Five

I HEARD Brodie moving about quite early, then he let himself out of the room.

I rose shortly after and dressed. I made notes in my notebook from our discoveries the day before, then went downstairs to the tavern.

The proprietress was there, customers already filling the tap room for breakfast before heading off for the races she had spoken of the night before.

"Yer husband has gone to see about a driver," she informed with a cheery greeting.

Husband. Did he still think of himself as that? I wondered.

"I've got a fresh pot of coffee on the cookstove."

I nodded. "Yes, please."

Brodie returned shortly after. He had arranged for a coach at the rail station to make the return trip to Sandringham.

He was matter-of-fact as I had seen him countless times before when making inquiries in a case. Nothing seemed to have changed...

"We need to go," he replied.

Brodie paid for the room and the meals, then escorted me from the tavern. The ride back to Sandringham was equally polite, and quiet.

It was very near nine o'clock in the morning when we arrived.

In parting the previous evening, Brodie had let Mr. Compton know that we would be returning.

The head steward at Sandringham met us on the front steps much like a gate-keeper with the keys to the kingdom and that impression of something very near resentment from the day before.

"How may we serve you today, sir?" he inquired with that aloof manner that was in fact most condescending.

"The conservatory is as you left it yesterday," he assured us.

Brodie thanked him, then made the request to speak with the head groundskeeper. I noted the man's surprise, then he replied, "Of course, I will advise Mr. Strangway. Is there a specific request?"

Brodie ignored the question. "Thank ye, sir," he politely told him instead. "We will meet him at the gardens at the far end of the manor."

"Of course, sir."

"Hopefully the footprints are still there," Brodie commented as we then set off to meet with the head groundskeeper.

Mr. Strangway arrived a short time later, escorted by Mr. Compton. The man most certainly was determined to oversee our every move.

Introductions were made and then Brodie once again thanked Mr. Compton for his assistance, dismissing him.

The house steward turned to Mr. Strangway and informed him that he would need to speak with him after he met with us. No doubt to question him regarding any inquiries we made.

Brodie waited until Mr. Compton had returned to the manor, then turned to the groundskeeper as we walked through the gardens to the location of those footprints we had seen the previous evening.

Along the way he commended the man on the gardens, along with several questions as I had seen him do countless times as he put the man at ease and built a certain level of cooperation with him, as Mr. Strangway had no doubt been cautioned about speaking with us.

In between, Brodie asked about the last night when the gentlemen were all present for a weekend of gaming, and perhaps a bit of hunting in the forest just beyond. Had the groundskeeper noticed anything afterward, perhaps one of the gentlemen partaking of a cigarette or taking a walk about?

"Oh, no, sir. The weather had set in and would have made it quite difficult. The gentlemen remained inside through the evening."

We eventually arrived near the base of those steps that led up to the suite of rooms Sir Collingwood had occupied during that 'gentlemen's weekend.'

"Who among yer staff would tend these gardens?" Brodie asked.

"Most usually that would be Ben McMasters and young Tim, one of the lads he's brought on. If they were needed elsewhere, then it would be meself and one of the other men. It's a sizable task, maintaining the gardens for Their Royal Highnesses."

Then, something that Brodie was also very accomplished at, his probing for information, his experience with other cases, as he pointed to the boot print in the mud at the base of the steps which had survived intact due to the warmth of the day and no additional rain through the night.

"It seems one of yer people might have recently attended this part of the gardens."

Mr. Roberts studied the print. "No, sir. Not since the rain set in. I've only just today been able to get the lads out and about their responsibilities here. With His Highness back in London for these few days, we will have the opportunity to clean and set the gardens aright before he returns. And ye can see, sir, the print is not of the sort of boot worn by me or the lads."

He gave it a closer inspection.

"This does have the look more of a gentleman's boot." He was thoughtful. "I suppose it's possible that one of them might have stepped out for a bit of fresh air or a smoke."

Might that 'bit of fresh air' or 'a smoke' have included the lady who had obviously also been present that weekend?

Brodie thanked him. "Ye've been most helpful."

"If there's nothing else, sir, I need to get on with my work while the sun is with us."

"Of course," Brodie replied. "We'll find our way back."

"And he will no doubt report our conversation to Mr. Compton," I added when he had gone.

"Aye," he replied as he studied the prints once more.

"We need to see where these prints lead. It might tell us something about what Sir Collingwood was about that night."

We set off and followed those prints through the gardens and then beyond to the edge of the forest. The tree cover and gorse were quite thick, which raised the obvious question— what would have taken Sir Collingwood into the forest that late night?

"It might be useful to split up," I suggested. There was somewhat of a path that led off in one direction.

Brodie nodded. "I'll continue in this other direction. Keep sight of the manor so not to get lost."

I headed off one way, Brodie in the other.

The forest was denser there as I followed the path that at times disappeared, then reappeared. However, the forest floor was covered with leaves and pine needles that made it impossible to know if there were any prints there.

As I continued, I was forced to push aside low hanging branches that had broken off—including juniper. Was it possible Sir Collingwood had come this way?

That question was answered as I found a boot print on the path where the undergrowth and forest debris thinned and exposed soft earth. Then another.

What was Sir Collingwood doing in the forest that last night? Was he merely out for a walk? Or had he come here to meet someone?

I pushed aside a thick branch of low-growing elder with those long, toothed leaves and that faint sweet smell that reminded me of the forest at Old Lodge, then suddenly stopped at the sight of the body before me or what was left of it, a leg that protruded from the undergrowth. And I was not alone.

There was much grunting and snorting, and that leg thrown about.

I had heard those sounds before a long time ago, the memory suddenly surfacing, and my stomach tightened as a dark shape suddenly appeared. The boar raised that massive head with bloodied tusks. Beady eyes stared back at me.

It seemed that I had found Sir Collingwood, or what was left of him.

I forced myself to think.

The knife that Munro had given me when I made my first travel along with the revolver that Brodie insisted I carry were both in my carpet bag. However, in order to retrieve either one would have immediately brought the beast down on me.

"Dinnae move," Brodie said in a quiet voice, somewhere very near.

I wondered if breathing was part of that. I then saw the sudden change in the boar's stance. It pawed the ground sending clumps of bloodied sod and flesh into the air, then charged.

The silence of the forest exploded in a series of loud shots as Brodie fired—once, twice, three times and still the boar charged.

It caught me at the knees and rolled me as he fired twice more, followed by the sound of thrashing through the elder brush just beyond where I lay. Then silence.

Brodie moved past me, followed that bloody path into the underbrush, then returned.

"Is it dead?" I barely recognized my own voice.

"Are ye hurt?" Brodie returned the revolver to the waist of his trousers. But I barely heard him.

"Is it dead?" I demanded.

"Are ye hurt?"

He was there, kneeling beside me, hands at my arms as if he would shake a response from me.

"No!" I shouted, then tried to push him away with that sudden need to get away from the blood and gore.

He held on. "Are ye certain yer not injured? Mikaela?" Urgent this time, pulling me back from the fear and the blood and gore.

I nodded. "I'm certain." Although my skirt had not fared as

well, and I realized just how dangerous the encounter had been at the long tear in the fabric, no doubt caused as the boar charged.

That dark gaze met mine, and I saw something else there— fear.

"Aye," he eventually replied. "Let's get ye on yer feet. We need to get back to the manor."

I glanced past him at the carcass of the boar, bloodied from bullet wounds along with remnants of that body nearby, those beady eyes still staring quite dead now.

I was wobbly and started to shake. Brodie pulled me against him.

"I've got ye."

He held onto me, his beard brushing my cheek.

"Ye are a troublesome baggage, Mikaela Forsythe." The hand that stroked my hair shook slightly.

"I've been told that."

We stood there for several moments, holding on to each other in the silence of the forest.

"Yer certain ye are all right?" he asked again. "Can ye stand?"

I assured him that I could, then glanced past him to that mutilated body.

"Sir Collingwood?"

"So, it would seem from what is left of him."

He went to the body then, crouched down, and made several observations in spite of the condition of the body.

"He's been dead verra likely since that night he was found to be missing. However, it would seem that the beast that attacked ye was not what killed him."

There was the distinct odor, the body already beginning to

decay. Or, what was left of it. It did seem that the boar wasn't particular about that.

He lifted the edge of Sir Collingwood's jacket. "Knife wounds, several of them, undoubtedly the cause of death. And then the body was left for the animals to have their way, perhaps with the hope it would never be found."

That changed everything as far as our inquiry was concerned.

"The body will need to be sent back to London," he said then as other sounds were heard, gradually coming nearer. No doubt staff from Sandringham at the sound of those shots being fired.

"We'll need to return to London as soon as possible."

Sir Collingwood's disappearance was no longer a case of a missing person who had taken himself off after a particularly interesting weekend of gambling in the company of His Royal Highness, and...others. Those stab wounds told a far different story.

His disappearance was now a murder investigation.

A local physician was requested in spite of the fact there was nothing to be done. Mr. Compton identified the remains as those of Sir Collingwood, then they were bound and placed in a plain wood coffin appropriated from the village blacksmith.

Several hours later, a handful of servants, including Mr. Compton, assembled at the steps of Sandringham Manor as we departed.

"His Royal Highness will need to be notified," he said in that reserved manner that all servants were obviously required to maintain—even with a body that had been discovered very near the manor.

"I will see that it is done," Brodie replied.

He sent a telegram to Sir Avery in London upon our arrival at the rail station. When the train arrived, the coffin was taken aboard. He then joined me in the compartment for the return to London.

We were the only ones in the compartment when the train departed. Several times I looked up to find that him watching me.

"Ye are a rare woman, Mikaela Forsythe."

I had heard that before, but after everything that had happened, I was left to wonder what it now meant, most particularly, for us.

Six

LONDON

A VAN and coach were waiting at St. Pancras station upon our arrival in spite of the late hour, along with instructions from the driver that he was to take us to the agency offices at the Tower.

"We will need to speak with the gentlemen who were there," Brodie informed Sir Avery as we met. "There is also the matter of someone who was at the manor house during that time whose name was not on the list you provided. A woman it seems."

Sir Avery studied my hastily written report. He finished it, then rubbed the bridge of his nose in that manner of someone who has perhaps not slept in a while and was now forced to deal with an even more difficult situation.

"His Royal Highness mentioned it and requested that the woman's name be left off the list. Not entirely unexpected considering past situations," he chose his words carefully. "Angeline Cotillard."

The actress!

"And now someone we are forced to deal with." Sir Avery added her name to the list and handed it back to Brodie.

He looked at me then. "The gentlemen who need to be questioned, difficult as that may be, may be more forthcoming with Mr. Brodie."

One of their own, man-to-man as it were, rather than with a woman, myself, in spite of my connection with the royal family. Or possibly because of it?

As Brodie and I had of each taking on an aspect of an investigation, there was something else that could be important.

"There might be something to be learned at Sir Collingwood's residence," I suggested. "Something mentioned to the servants or something left about that could provide information."

"Sir Collingwood was a very meticulous person. I doubt you will find anything, but I do understand," Sir Avery replied.

"Quite obviously in consideration of Sir Collingwood's position with the Queen's Privy Council as well as his position of Lord High Admiral, we will not be able to keep this development unknown," he continued.

"But I would prefer to be able to control when it is known and the extent of the circumstances that we will also allow to be known, in order to avoid any hint of a scandal. Therefore, I will be speaking with each of the guests who were present at Sandringham, myself, including the Prince of Wales, and making them aware of this development.

"As for making inquiries at Sir Collingwood's personal residence, Brodie, it might be best for you to accompany Lady Forsythe, in order to avoid any hesitation on the part of his servants. I will provide a letter providing you access which I will send round."

And a final instruction.

"As much as possible, it would be best not to mention this latest development to anyone. It will, of course, come out in due time, but I would prefer that it be a time of our choosing, once we know more about it, in the interest of keeping control of the narrative. Is that understood?"

Control of the narrative. That was an interesting way of putting it, I thought.

"Aye," Brodie replied.

I could tell that he was not at all pleased with the turn of events. It did seem that we might be engaged in this with the Agency for an extended period of time.

Sir Avery nodded. "I will make contact when arrangements are in place. Where may I contact you?" He looked first at Brodie, then at me.

"We can be reached at the office on the Strand," Brodie replied.

We.

I did wonder what that might mean now, with everything that had happened. Brodie accompanied me to Mayfair, then continued on to the office I presumed. Of course, it was possible that he had taken accommodations elsewhere during the past few months.

I told myself that it shouldn't matter.

There were changes in the office on the Strand. I noticed them as soon as I arrived the next morning.

The well-worn signage on the third floor that advertised available office space along with health tonics, legal services, and the somewhat vague reference *'personal services at reasonable rates'* that raised obvious questions, had all been removed, along with the smaller sign nearer the street that had read:

A. Brodie, Private Inquiries

In truth, I had some difficulty finding it that first time as it was quite small. The small sign was all that the building's landlord allowed. As for legal services, that was self-explanatory, although I had never seen anyone coming or going at those other offices on the third floor, which did raise the obvious question just who, if anyone, was occupying those offices.

There was now new signage that read:

Brodie and Associates, Private Inquiries.

That was interesting, I thought. The sign was brass with raised letters and quite tasteful, something one might see in Mayfair or at St. James.

"The rents will undoubtedly increase. I've had Munro inquire about other places where I might open an office."

"Miss Forsythe," Mr. Cavendish, who was also known as the Mudger to those on the streets of the East End, greeted me with a large smile as he paddled out from under the alcove.

He lived in the alcove, most of the time, and had become a good friend as well as a source of clues in previous inquiry cases. He had been injured in a past accident some years before that took both of his legs. He now wheeled about on a wood platform with amazing speed and agility, often dodging among trams and carriages on the street.

It would have been too easy to feel sorry for him. He would not have tolerated it. In truth, I regarded him as a trusted friend.

"Good to see you. It hasn't been right around here without you," he added pointedly, with a look over at Brodie.

Rupert, the hound, accompanied him and now stopped a few feet away. He sat down with head cocked in a way that suggested he wasn't at all certain who I might be. There was also the possibility that he wasn't at all pleased with me, his ears flattened, and then there was that sideways glance.

"I see there have been some changes." I indicated the new sign.

"And not a word to Mr. Brodie other than the people who came round to make the change," he replied. "And let us know as well that the building is to be painted."

He was obviously not pleased about it.

"I suppose I'll have to find someplace else to live with the hound once the new owner comes round. Won't be easy. Most people are put off by him."

Rupert still hadn't approached, as if he didn't know what to make of me after all the time I'd been away.

The hound and I had shared past adventures in two inquiry cases. In fact, it could very definitely be said that he had saved my life on one particular occasion.

I had acquired a love of hounds as a child, his predecessor also named Rupert, and had a fondness for him.

Now, I knelt at the sidewalk and spoke to him. He immediately launched himself toward me and would have bowled me over if Brodie hadn't reached out a hand to support me.

"The beast hasn't been right for months," Mr. Cavendish explained. "Surly as the devil. Yer the only one who seems to have a way with him."

"We understand each other," I replied as I finally stood. Rupert immediately flattened himself across the toe of my boot and angled a sad-eyed look up at me.

"Come along then," I told the hound and headed for the stairs that led to the office on the second floor with Brodie.

It had not changed since I was last there some months before. The chalkboard on the far wall still contained the notes I had made on the last inquiry case we took together.

"I keep forgetting to clean the board. It was something ye took care of when ye were here makin' yer notes about a particular case..."

That dark gaze met mine.

"That is more than obvious," I replied.

I picked up a small piece of chalk in the chalk rail.

"It does appear that I will need more chalk if I'm to make them."

I heard the distinct sound as one of the desk drawers was pulled open. He came up behind me, and held out a new piece of chalk.

"I could show you the proper way to make the notes," I told him. I didn't trust myself to look over my shoulder at him. "The order is chronological and usually best as one piece of information often leads to another. It's really quite simple."

"Yer far better at such things. Ye can hardly read my writing," he replied, a bit of an exaggeration. This from a man who had taught himself how to read and write, and had at one time written lengthy police reports.

The jangle of the office telephone interrupted. Brodie cursed softly as he lifted the earpiece. An hour later, a courier from the Agency brought round a sealed message along with that letter Sir Avery had spoken of.

As for our visit to the Collingwood residence, it had been arranged for us to call on the residence at one o'clock in the afternoon, which was several hours away.

"I want to speak with Templeton beforehand," I

announced after the courier had left. "I thought that it might be useful to learn if she knows anything about Angeline Cotillard, as they share the same profession and have both toured extensively."

Brodie agreed. "Take the hound with ye."

There it was. That protective nature of his that had led to that nasty argument and our parting months earlier.

It had not resolved itself then. Now, it seemed necessary, if there was to be any reconciliation, even if it was limited to our partnership in inquiry cases.

"The theater is near and safe enough this time of the day," I added, remembering something of our companion's words of wisdom during our initial trip to Norfolk—*compromise*.

"Aye," he finally replied. "Perhaps ye are right. I suppose it is safe enough."

I did wonder if I had heard that correctly and looked up from across the desk. It was a small thing under the circumstances. However, no small thing for Angus Brodie.

I would have made a comment but decided against. It was best to simply take that small victory.

"I will meet you back here to make our appointment with the servants at Sir Collingwood's residence."

I then put my notebook and pen in the bag, and left.

As I made the short ride to the Theater Royal, I wondered if my friend had acquired any new pets. She did have a penchant for bringing them with her to the theater. Ziggy came to mind, a four-and-a half-foot iguana that had been a gift from an admirer on one of her tours.

Her admirer spoke no English, she spoke no Spanish. She was forced to learn a few key phrases in Spanish since it appeared that Ziggy only understood that language.

After more than one performance that I attended with

Ziggy on the loose, she could be heard attempting to persuade him back to the captivity of her dressing room with words she'd learned courtesy of one of the stage hands at the time.

It rapidly became apparent that the vocabulary was quite colorful and perhaps not what Templeton intended. In any event, Ziggy was finally persuaded back to her dressing room with...red roses.

I'd had luncheon with Templeton after my return from safari. When she completed her current commitment at the Theatre Royal she was to depart for Europe. She would be gone for several months and had chatted on about the play she would be performing, her fellow cast members, then none too subtly slipped in a question about Brodie.

It seemed that she had seen Munro from time to time while I was gone. In his stoic manner, much like Brodie's, he had shared nothing of our difficulty. Which, of course, left her to imagine all sorts of things.

"*I will not ask you about your relationship with Brodie,*" she had announced at the time, and I had thanked her.

"*Unless of course you wish to talk about it?*" She dropped the too obvious hint.

I did not, and we had moved on to other bits and pieces of theater conversation.

It did seem that she was not particularly looking forward to the tour this time.

"It does become tiring, and then there is all the competition from other actors and only so many productions. I have managed to save a substantial amount of my earnings. A girl must always have another plan waiting in the wings, don't you think?"

Now as I arrived at the theatre, I hoped that Templeton

74

might know Angeline Cotillard or at least be able to tell me something about her.

"The woman is quite despicable!" Templeton announced as we met in her dressing room.

That was certainly getting off to a most interesting start. And Ziggy had yet to make an appearance. Still, it was not wise to linger.

"What of Angeline's personal life?"

Was she married? What was known about her family? Rumored lovers?

"She will sleep with anyone in order to get a part in a play, and I have heard that she has even slept with the president of France! She has absolutely no scruples."

I thought that was a bit like the pot calling the kettle black, however in the interest of our current inquiry case I thought it best not to point that out.

"What else do you know about her? Anything that might be useful?"

Templeton's eyes widened. "Is she a suspect in a case?"

"Merely someone who might know something about a private matter."

"In other words, you cannot tell me."

Those were the words.

She sat back in the chair at her dressing table with a thoughtful expression, the very image of Cleopatra, whom she had portrayed to great success.

"She would have everyone believe that she is descended from royalty," she began. "Some distant, long-dead relative."

"In France?" That did seem somewhat risky, given the purges and the new republic that had been created.

"Some Hungarian prince or other. It changes from time to time. I suppose that it depends on whom she is trying to impress. I have also heard that her mother worked the streets and her father, the man who some said might be her father, was merely one of her customers. She was then raised by another woman in the theater. She has been kept by more men than you have fingers on both hands."

It did seem as if we had wandered into an area of speculation, rumor, or gossip, that didn't tell me a great deal.

Yet it did seem that Angeline was an enterprising sort. The men of her 'acquaintance' were rumored to include the Prince of Wales, the very same host of that weekend of gaming and other 'sporting.' But what did that mean?

I did consider the fact that Templeton was rumored to have once held that lofty position with Bertie.

"The woman is absolutely unscrupulous!" she continued, on a roll, as they say.

"There are even rumors that one of her lovers died under suspicious circumstances over a piece of jewelry or a precious stone or some such that was quite valuable. He died while in the midst of..."

I understood her meaning.

"Does your current inquiry case involve her?" she asked with no effort to disguise her curiosity. "And you are now back with Brodie?"

Not exactly subtle. It was amazing how she managed to slip in a personal question. The truth was, I didn't know where Brodie and I stood.

I explained that we were working together on the present case which didn't answer that one question and didn't fool her for a moment.

"Of course," she replied.

As I moved her along in the conversation, she was able to

tell me a story of a play in Paris where she had opened just after Angeline closed a play of her own.

"The dressing room absolutely reeked of cigarette smoke. It's the sort that you smoke from time to time," she added. "However, it was so strong that it wilted the flowers she had received.

"The play was *Salome*, quite disgusting. The woman played an exotic dancer and had no reservation about removing all her clothes! Oh, and she has this peculiar little man who goes everywhere with her. It does make one wonder about her taste in companions. He was quite small..."

A woman who preferred those Turkish cigarettes, had performed in the play *Salome* which had been banned in London, would take her clothes off when she portrayed an exotic dancer, and had a rather small companion who went everywhere with her.

I now knew somewhat more about Angeline Cotillard than when I arrived. However, it was too soon to know what any of it might have had to do with Sir Collingwood's murder.

I met Brodie back at the office, and went over everything Templeton had shared with me.

"It could be useful," he commented. "If she was there as a guest of His Highness, is there a connection to Sir Collingwood? Or was his death merely a random act."

"Random?"

"The sort of guests who were there are rich and powerful men. His Highness is fond of horse racing and we were told that he usually had a horse participating in the local races.

"I contacted Mr. Conner. He knows people in and about racing here in London where there are usually enormous bets made. A great deal of money at stake has a way of drawing all sorts. With the races that were to begin, it is possible that Sir

Collingwood might have been meeting with someone regarding a bet."

"Or," I suggested, "in the wrong place at the wrong time?"

He put on his long coat as I finished making my notes on the board from my meeting with Templeton.

"Perhaps."

Waverly House at St. James's had been in Sir Collingwood's family for over two hundred years.

It was a two-story brick manor with a slate roof that sat at the edge of St. James's Park, and very near Admiralty House and the official Admiralty offices where he also had an office for his work as part of the Queen's Privy Council.

We were met at the entrance by Sir Collingwood's head butler. He had been notified to expect our arrival and, by his demeanor, it appeared that he had been informed about Sir Collingwood's death.

"I have been instructed to answer whatever questions that I may be able, and to make the other servants available to you as well," he informed us in that formal manner of one who had also served in the Queen's Navy, and then retired to his current position.

We were then introduced to his housekeeper, Mrs. Burton, and his personal valet, Mr. Long.

After meeting them, Brodie asked if it would be possible to meet with each one individually in the library adjacent to the parlor where I settled in to take notes.

His questions for Mr. Jamison, the head butler, were initially met with some hesitation which I attributed to that natural loyalty of a servant, along with that military demeanor.

"Sir, I respect yer position and any instructions ye may have been given," Brodie told him. "However, we have been sent by

Sir Avery Stanton of the Special Services at the request of His Highness the Prince of Wales.

"This letter will advise ye of the importance of the matter as well as authorization for ye to cooperate." He handed him the letter. "Ye may discuss this with Sir Avery, or perhaps ye wish me to inform His Highness that ye refuse to cooperate in the matter?"

"I understand. I will assist in any way that I can."

If anyone was in a position to know Sir Collingwood's schedule, appointments, as well as any unusual situation— aside from any situations that pertained to his work as Lord High Admiral of the Navy—it would have been this man, who we learned had been in service with Sir Collingwood for very near twenty years.

Apparently, there was nothing out of the ordinary prior to Sir Collingwood's trip to Sandringham to join the Prince of Wales and his other guests.

His schedule was full of appointments that Mr. Jamison oversaw as far as his travel back and forth to the Admiralty offices and providing any notes that were send round from staff there.

"He had been most determined to clear his schedule for those few days. It did seem to be a much-needed respite and he was most anxious to be off to Sandringham."

Sir Collingwood had traveled there by rail the day prior to his Royal Highness's arrival, after changing his plans due to other arrangements that needed to be made.

I knew from my own travels that changes did occur from time to time, and certainly for a man of Sir Collingwood's position that would not have been unusual.

Yet, a day ahead? And other arrangements?

I made note of everything discussed, including questions that arose as a result as Brodie continued with the usual questions in an inquiry case.

Did Sir Collingwood seem upset or distracted by anything?

Was there anything unusual about this particular gathering at Sandringham?

Did he perhaps mention anything that he was concerned about? Or a recent difficulty?

Then, one final question, of an extremely private nature but necessary.

Did Sir Collingwood ever mention someone by the name of Angeline Cotillard?

"A woman?" he remarked with some surprise, then replied. "No, not that I'm aware, sir."

Brodie thanked him. He then asked to meet with each of the other servants in turn.

Each one was asked a variation of the same questions with much the same answers. Then we met with Sir Collingwood's housekeeper.

Miss Burrell was somewhere near fifty years of age, tall, thin, with pinched features and a formal demeanor that reminded me of Mr. Jamison's rigid, military bearing. She had been in Sir Collingwood's employ for ten years.

Brodie deferred to me in questioning her, as had become quite useful in our previous inquiries.

I proceeded to ask much the same questions as before, but with a different purpose as I inquired if there had been any recent changes in the household, perhaps a member of the staff that might have departed?

Did Sir Collingwood seem preoccupied in any way? What about social engagements? Or entertainments that he had scheduled? And possible guests?

The responses were all the same, and he had not entertained guests in the weeks leading up to his departure for
Sandringham.

She hesitated when I inquired if there was any change in
the usual routine of the household.

"Was it something he said?" Brodie added.

She angled a look toward the hall just beyond those double
doors.

"He told me there was no need to make my usual purchases
at the grocer as he would be quite busy with work at the Admiralty office."

That didn't seem particularly unusual to me. There was
another look to the hallway.

"And he gave us our weekly pay before he left to meet with
the other gentlemen for that weekend. I wouldn't have thought
anything of it, but when I opened the envelope, he had paid me
for the full month. When I spoke with Mr. Fields, his driver,
about it. He had received the same."

Most interesting.

"There's more," I quickly added, when she had gone. "I
found Sir Collingwood's accounts ledger in a drawer of the
desk.

"Ye just happened to see it?"

"I thought it might be useful...perhaps unusual amounts
drawn on his bank, that sort of thing."

"Go on."

"In addition to paying their wages in advance, there were
entries for all of the household accounts. He paid everything in
advance, as if he wouldn't return for some time."

Or at all? I thought. Brodie had the same thought. I did
know how his thoughts worked.

The last person we spoke with was Sir Collingwood's

driver, Mr. Fields, who would have been responsible for taking him back and forth to the Admiralty offices, or any other location.

While we waited for him to arrive, I made my usual notes, then set aside my notebook and pen as I moved about the library.

It gave me the opportunity to observe things beyond the questions that were asked, and had provided valuable information in the past.

Sir Collingwood's selection of books on the shelves behind his desk were of the usual sort, I supposed, for a man who had lived his life in service with the Royal Navy.

There were several books regarding the history of warfare in places such as the Mediterranean, that included Roman and Greek sea battles, along with several maps, one in particular over the slate fireplace.

It was most interesting, with locations marked with images of ancient sailing vessels and barges. Not unusual, I supposed, for a man of Sir Collingwood's long history with the Royal Navy or his position as Lord High Admiral.

A handful of those locations were ports and places that I had explored along the coast of Malta, the Black Sea when traveling to Budapest, and the Mediterranean to Alexandria more recently. Once the driver arrived, Brodie asked questions regarding Sir Collingwood's schedule and any recent appointments before leaving London for that weekend of gaming.

Were there any unusual destinations the past few weeks? Any additional passengers he might have taken on at Sir Collingwood's request? Perhaps something said by way of instructions he was given that might have seemed out of the ordinary?

Mr. Fields's responses revealed nothing out of the ordinary over the past several weeks. However, when questions about any unusual behavior, he also mentioned that he had been paid for the full month rather than the usual weekly pay.

As I listened to Brodie's questions, I poked at bits and pieces of paper among the ashes that had not fully burned with the toe of my boot. I knelt for a closer look, sifting through the usual sticky residue that was left behind from a fire in a coal stove.

I poked about the ash with my fingers and discovered bits and pieces of paper left behind after the fire had burned. I continued to dig and poke about, and discovered a half-dozen good-sized and smaller pieces of paper that had survived the fire.

"What have ye there?" Brodie asked after Mr. Fields left.

"It seems that Sir Collingwood burned papers in the fireplace."

He came round the desk where I knelt with soot-stained fingers. He leaned down and frowned at the smudged and stained pieces of...

What? Merely some household trash? Or had Sir Collingwood simply cleared his desk before leaving for a few days?

"It could be useful," Brodie commented. "Best bring wot ye can find and we'll see if it reveals anything important."

I gently pressed the fragile pieces of paper between the pages in my notebook, tucked it into my bag, and dusted off my hands as Mr. Jamison returned to inquire if there was anything else we needed.

Brodie didn't question him regarding the information the housekeeper had given us. If he was aware of any other plans Sir Collingwood might have had after returning from Sandringham, he had chosen not to speak of it. Nor had he mentioned the advanced payment for several weeks' employment.

That might mean something in itself, or nothing at all. However, I was most eager to see what those burnt pieces of paper might tell us.

Seven

WE RETURNED to the office on the Strand with the information we'd learned as well as those pieces of paper that I carefully laid out on the blotter at Brodie's desk.

"Can ye make anything of it?" Brodie asked after I had been at it for some time.

"It's a bit like a jigsaw puzzle with a good many pieces missing that were completely burnt to ash in the fireplace," I replied as I bent over the desk.

It was a tedious, painfully slow process as the note was handwritten and handling the fragile pieces caused the dry and brittle paper to crumble while the letters on larger pieces made no sense.

"It might it be useful to make a list of the letters and words on the chalkboard," he suggested.

We had often discovered a clue in that manner, standing back, looking at information we had gathered, attempting to determine what it all meant.

However, this time, he stood at the board while I attempted to read the letters on the bits and pieces of paper.

It reminded me how we had worked together in the past—trading ideas, my note-making, the way he looked at things with his experience from his work with the MET, and from the streets, combined with what I was able to contribute.

However, this might be the exception, I thought, as I looked up at the board at the random letters.

"Nothing makes any sense. It's like some other language," he commented.

I stood and came round the desk, then frowned as I stared at the chalkboard.

"What is it?"

"Something..." I replied. Yet I had no idea what it was.

He handed me the chalk and I began to rearrange letters.

I added one set of letters to another, then started all over again.

"Rue Miron."

"French?" he stared at the board. "Do ye know what it means?"

"It's a street in Paris, in the Montparnasse Arrondissement."

"And ye just happen to know of it."

I ignored the sarcasm. "Linnie and I did attend school in Paris." I didn't elaborate on that, as I had been to the district several times in my wanderings about Paris when I should have been at my studies.

"There appears to be a name," I added to distract any further questions about Paris.

"I suppose that ye recognize that as well."

"It's not French, possibly Hungarian—Szábo."

It meant nothing to me.

What more had been in the rest of that handwritten letter that had gone up in flames at Sir Collingwood's residence?

"It might have been an official communication, considering his position with Admiralty," I suggested. "Particularly if he was to depart for Sandringham for several days. But this is not the quality of official stationery. It's more the sort like my note pad. And why burn it?"

Brodie studied what I had managed to extract from those seemingly random bits and pieces of paper that had survived the fire.

"It would seem that Sir Collingwood didn't want to risk the servants or anyone else seein' it. That, along with the fact that he paid the servants a full month in advance..." he added.

"His housekeeper said that he told her not to make purchases at the grocers. Is it possible that he didn't intend to return?"

"It would seem so," Brodie replied. "Taking care of things before he planned to be gone. And there is that street name in Paris."

What did it mean? Perhaps someone he knew in Paris? Some time away? Or was it something else?

And what did that name mean? Who was Szábo?

There was someone who might know, someone who was deeply connected to the immigrant community in the East End —Herr Schmidt, owner of the German Gymnasium.

We had contacted him in a previous inquiry case and he was able, somewhat reluctantly, to provide valuable information. However, persuading him was a somewhat complicated endeavor.

Quid pro quo came to mind. A favor granted for a favor requested.

The two-story German Gymnasium was in St. Pancras, between the St. Pancras and Kings Cross railway stations. It had been built several decades earlier with contributions from the German community in the East End.

On the second floor was the area used for women's exercises and gymnastics. The National Olympian association used the gymnasium for training.

The ground floor contained a boxing ring along with an area for providing lessons with rapiers and swords.

I had brought Lily here for lessons, due to her insatiable curiosity for Montgomery ancestral weapons at Sussex Square. She had excelled in her training, surpassing several levels with at least three different blades.

Her favorite was the *falcion*. She had trained with it. However, the reality that it was too large and quite cumbersome as far as something she might carry with her when she was out and about was soon obvious.

I had recently learned that Munro had provided her with a folding knife and had proceeded to provide her lessons on the best use of it.

"I should probably have one as well," my great-aunt had commented when Lily had excitedly informed me about the lessons. "A woman can never be too careful, you know," my great-aunt had whispered. "Rapists. It seems there has been an increase in such attacks about the city."

Why was I not surprised?

I carried a knife in my bag that Munro had provided when I first set off on my world travels, along with lessons in the use of.

The thought was initially ridiculous. An eighty-six-year-old woman who was no taller than Lily taught how to use a knife?

Yet, this was a woman who had fought off a street thief with her umbrella and inflicted substantial damage until the constables arrived.

I did reason with her that she should forget the knife and rely on her umbrella in the future. My recommendation had fallen on deaf ears.

Merely the week before, she had showed me the blade that Munro had provided and she had already had several lessons. London thieves were not safe.

Brodie and I arrived at the gymnasium. As we approached the front counter with that display board behind that listed weekly classes I noticed they had added women's defense classes.

"That could be dangerous," Brodie commented.

I ignored the sarcasm. I was quite well accomplished in the art of self-defense and it had been quite useful in the past.

I asked the attendant at the counter if we might speak with Herr Schmidt. He picked up the handset with one of those speaking tubes, a new addition since we were last there.

There was a brief conversation in German. Brodie gave our names, and that conversation ended.

"You will please wait," we were told.

Herr Schmidt eventually made his appearance. He was portly with short greying hair that stood on end. A long, bushy handlebar mustache extended past his chin, while thickly muscled arms were evident beneath the shirt he'd tucked into rough work pants. Tall boots reached to his knees.

He had immigrated to London over thirty years earlier with his family and then established the gymnasium. In spite of his size, he was proficient with a rapier and several other weapons, and was rumored to have once been belonged to the Hessian military in Germany.

He was well-known in the German community, acquired information from others, and had been a source of valuable information in the past.

"Mr. Brodie and Lady Forsythe," he greeted us with that thick German accent that remained after all the years in London.

"I would ask what do I owe the pleasure, as you say? But I know it is not a social call. Yes?" He escorted us to his office at the back of the main floor of the gymnasium.

Rather than engage in lengthy conversation, Brodie laid the note that I had deciphered on the desk in front of him.

"What do ye know about this?"

The expression on Herr Schmidt's face changed. Not usually congenial, nevertheless he had been pleasant enough in the past. As I say, in the past.

He shoved the paper back across the desk, and sat back in his chair.

"I think you play a dangerous game, Herr Brodie, and dangerous for a lady," he added with a look over at me.

"Do ye recognize it?" Brodie insisted. "Is it a name? An organization? What can you tell us?"

"Szábo," he spat out with that heavy accent once again and in a way that said he recognized it. "It is a man. Not one you want to know."

"Then you know who he is," I replied.

"I know what is said about him."

"What would that be?" Brodie inquired.

Herr Schmidt didn't answer. Instead, he reached behind him and opened a cabinet door. He removed a bottle and uncorked it. He poured a glass, then a second one and pushed it across to Brodie.

"Drink, Herr Brodie. Then, we will talk." He downed the drink, what I assumed was very likely schnapps, a favorite in the German community.

Brodie did the same, then set the glass back on top of the desk somewhat sharply.

If the situation wasn't quite so serious, it would have been amusing. Two men, each staring the other down, in some ancient medieval male ritual.

"What else do ye know?" Brodie continued.

Herr Schmidt angled a look toward the door. Brodie closed it, then took the chair beside me. Herr Schmidt then filled the glasses once more.

"The Hungarian." He took a drink of Schnapps.

"Then ye do know him."

Eventually Herr Schmidt replied. "We will trade. I will tell you what I know, and you will perhaps provide something..."

Brodie nodded. "If the information you have is worth it."

"You would not have come to me if it was not worth it, Herr Brodie."

There it was again, that squaring off with one another.

"What is it that ye want?"

Herr Schmidt slowly smiled. "My wife's brother has been trying to come to England for some time. There has been some difficulty here. His name is Karl Schneider. He is a butcher in one of the northern districts in Frankfurt. He can be reached there."

Brodie nodded. "I will do what I can to help him."

"I will contact him and let him know," Schmidt replied, then continued. "Szábo left Hungary a long time ago. Now, his home is wherever he is well paid. You understand?"

"France?" I suggested.

Schmidt shrugged. "France, Spain, Germany, wherever there is money to be had. You understand, Herr Brodie?"

"A soldier of fortune?" I had heard the term before.

There was another shrug. "Not exactly a soldier. He does

not command an army or a group of others like him. He puts people together for a price...a very high price."

"What sort of people?"

"Those who know things and those who want to know, those who have something that could be worth a great deal and those who would like to purchase."

"Secrets?"

"Ja, information, for those who are willing to pay a great deal of money."

I exchanged a look with Brodie.

"Who would be willing to pay such large sums...?"

The answer was there—any one of a handful of foreign governments where there had been unrest in recent years.

"What sort of information?" I asked Brodie as our driver pulled away from the sidewalk in front of the gymnasium. "For what purpose?"

My thinking had a tendency to go toward bank robbery, stealing of investment bonds, or perhaps even stealing the crown jewels as had been attempted in the past.

"Perhaps nothing as obvious as the crown jewels." I looked over at him. "A man of Sir Collingwood's position might have access to information that could be important."

And he had then been killed for it. We needed to find out exactly what had happened.

"Will you try to assist Herr Schmidt's brother-in-law?" I asked after we left.

"I will try. He didn't however mention what the difficulty was. I will need to be careful with that."

"Might Mr. Dooley be able to assist?" He had worked with Brodie in the past when he was at the MET, and had now achieved the position of detective.

He nodded. "Perhaps."

I heard the hesitation, and with good reason after his experience with former Chief Inspector Abberline during our previous inquiry case. Brodie's broken ribs had healed according to Munro, but he still carried the scar over his left eye from that encounter.

"*Teuch*, ye ken?" he replied when I inquired after my return from my travel with my great-aunt and Lily.

"He's tough," he translated the Gaelic word. "He's had to be with our time on the streets, and...other things."

He had not explained the last of it. There was no need. I heard it in his voice, those other things, the losses he'd been through.

As for the aftermath of the case? Brodie had not shared any of it with me. It was part of that distance between us after my return. Our exchanges were distant, polite, only marginally improved with the case we were now to pursue together.

Still, I knew that something had irrevocably changed.

I did, however, learn from Munro that, after the closing of the case, the Chief Inspector had been immediately suspended from his position over his treatment of Brodie. An official investigation was pending over the brutal beating Brodie received and his incarceration in Scotland Yard, as well as Abberline's interference in the inquiry case into the murder of Ellie Sutton, and Stephen Matthews ten years earlier.

Abberline was presently awaiting trial on multiple charges at Scotland Yard, the very same place where he had Brodie imprisoned. I personally felt there was no one more deserving.

As for a conversation regarding the case or our parting afterward, there had been no opportunity. Or at least none that he was willing to have with me.

He had been courteous, almost as it was in the begging

with the first inquiry case we shared. There was a distance between us now that I wasn't certain could be overcome.

I had spent the past months saddened, then angry that he could not understand the reasons I had continued with the previous case no matter the risk rather than see him unfairly prosecuted. He would have done no less.

In the past few days, things between us had almost seemed as they were when we worked so well together, even though there was still that distance. As if there were an invisible wall he kept between us. Although, more than once, I had sensed there was something he wanted to say, yet did not.

"I will send round a message for Dooley and see what he might be able to learn about Herr Schmidt's brother-in-law."

Our driver made our way across London toward the Tower.

Then he added, "Perhaps with the information we now have, Sir Avery will be able to continue with others in the investigation, and we may both carry on with other things."

There it was again, that barrier.

I had to admit that I wouldn't have minded being released from my agreement with Sir Avery—that other piece of Brodie's anger toward me. Although, it would also bring to an end our work on the case, and perhaps our personal relationship as well?

Eight

THE TOWER, LONDON

UNLIKE PREVIOUS OCCASIONS and in spite of the fact that we had no set appointment, we were not forced to wait to see Sir Avery upon our arrival. It was further emphasis as to the seriousness of the case.

Alex Sinclair met us in the hallway outside of his office. "You have information?"

Brodie nodded. "Aye. What of Sir Avery's inquiries with the other gentlemen who were present at Sandringham?"

"He has met with all of them, including the Prince of Wales, and only just returned. He will be most anxious to hear what you have learned in the matter. He also has spoken with the physician who inspected the body."

What was left of it, I thought with a shiver at the memory of that encounter in the forest at the royal estate.

"There were several knife wounds. However, it seems that the fatal wound was across the throat." Alex explained as he escorted us to Sir Avery's office.

Sir Avery rose from behind his desk as we entered. His

expression was unreadable for the most part and gave none of his thoughts away. He was the epitome of the perfect master of discretion or, as my great-aunt had said of him, the perfect sort to be a spy—completely unassuming in appearance, short in height, with features that would never draw attention except for that gaze that seemed to see everything.

And according to her as well, behind that unassuming 'common man' appearance was a ruthless demeanor and unwavering loyalty to Queen and country.

"There is a reason he was chosen to lead this new agency," she had said, surprising me as there were few who supposedly knew about it.

"Of course, spying on one's enemies is nothing new," she had continued at the time. *"It's been going on for centuries in one form or another. And the fact that the Queen has this secret group to gather information is nothing new either. It all began with her marriage to Prince Albert. He was German, you know. It was no secret there were concerns about the alliance and the need to keep tabs on what was going on not only in Germany, but in other countries as well.*

"Politics, my dear," she had added. *"It is said our great ancestor was quite good at it. Of course, in the eleventh century, if there were enemies, one simply had their heads cut off. You have to admit, gruesome as that was, it did effectively resolve quarrels."*

"You have information from your inquiries of Sir Collingwood's household staff?" Sir Avery now asked.

Brodie went over our initial meeting with the servants, the questions, and their responses.

"It did seem there was nothing out of the ordinary in the man's behavior, no unusual appointments, no unknown callers he might have met with. Miss Forsythe did, however, learn something curious from his housekeeper."

There it was again, as if we were merely associates in the business of making inquiries. I forced back the anger that would have been far too easy to indulge as I referred to my notes.

"The woman did mention that before leaving for Sandringham, Sir Collingwood had given each of the servants their weekly envelopes."

"Not necessarily unusual, as he was to be gone for several days," Sir Avery pointed out.

"However, on this occasion he paid each of them a full month's wage," I added. "He also instructed his housekeeper not to make her usual purchases at the grocer, and a ledger I found at his desk indicated that he had paid all of his bills well in advance. It would seem that he was planning on being gone for some time, or possibly closing his residence."

Sir Avery frowned as he paced the narrow space beside the desk.

"I called on a friend of mine in the theater," I added. "She is well acquainted with Angeline Cotillard, the woman who was a guest that weekend."

I went over everything Templeton had shared with me.

"It seems that she travels with a man, whom she described to me."

Sir Avery nodded. "That could be important. Is there anything else?"

Brodie looked over at me.

"A note was discovered that Sir Collingwood had apparently attempted to destroy at his residence at some point in time before leaving for Sandringham. Miss Forsythe was able to retrieve some of the information," he provided.

"What was in the note?"

I handed him my note where I had deciphered those odd bits and pieces that we retrieved from the fireplace.

"It was badly burned, only a few remnants remained. It was handwritten."

He studied the note.

"Szábo?" He read the name I had written there.

"There was also a street name in Paris."

He looked up.

"In the Montparnasse."

"We then spoke with a man in the German community," Brodie informed him. "It seems that Szábo is known as someone who accommodates certain arrangements. Herr Schmidt has agreed to learn whatever else he can, in exchange for a favor."

"What might that be?" Sir Avery inquired.

"It seems that his brother-in-law has been denied entry into the country," Brodie explained.

"And he would like for us to look the other way in exchange for information he might be able to provide about this person, Szábo?" Sir Avery concluded with a frown. "Does the brother-in-law have a name?"

Brodie provided him the information, then inquired about Sir Avery's meetings with the other guests who were at Sandringham the night Sir Collingwood disappeared.

"It seems that no one saw or heard anything unusual during their stay, most particularly the night that Sir Collingwood disappeared," he replied.

"Do ye believe them?"

Sir Avery frowned. "It is in their best interest to tell the truth. It seems that Sir Collingwood participated in the gaming along with the others that evening, then retired early."

And he had then left the manor to meet with someone after leaving the other gentlemen. Sir Avery explained when it was discovered that he was gone, it was assumed that he had returned to London.

"From what the other guests shared, the woman was there to provide entertainment of some sort," he continued. "She is an acquaintance of the Prince of Wales which means that this must be handled with all discretion."

Sir Avery paced the narrow space between his desk and the wall with a map of the world.

"Paris," he commented. "Whatever else was in that note, Sir Collingwood obviously didn't want anyone to know of it."

He was thoughtful for several long moments.

"It that all?" Brodie said.

"Not quite, Mr. Brodie. You and Lady Forsythe will need to go to Paris to try to determine what that burned note meant."

"There is no need for the both of us," Brodie protested. "I can make the inquiries necessary..."

It was obvious that he had no desire for us to continue further. I did admit that I had hoped that the information we'd learned would be the end of it, and hopefully the 'agreement' that I'd made with Sir Avery would be fulfilled.

"This case, and the potential implications for the Crown because of Sir Collingwood's position, require the utmost discretion to see those responsible brought to justice." He held a hand up when Brodie would have protested further.

"Your working arrangement is perfect for this. You will appear to be husband and wife with the excuse that you are traveling on holiday or perhaps intending to visit family. Lady Forsythe has spent considerable time in France, and Paris in particular. That could be of enormous help in this.

"Not only that," he continued. "She speaks the language. This will allow you to move about and make inquiries that perhaps others cannot. You have my answer Mr. Brodie, Lady Forsythe. You will be prepared to leave in the morning for Dover for travel to Calais and then Paris. Mr. Sinclair will accompany you to Dover from the rail station and will provide you with all travel information.

"You will also need travel documents. Mr. Sinclair will arrange for that, as well as the appropriate currency that you will need while in the city. Obviously, the address in the Montparnasse is a place to start.

"Hopefully you will be able to learn something there that may provide answers to this matter." He looked from Brodie to me. "Under no circumstances are you to reveal the real reason you will be in Paris. Do you have any questions?"

After leaving his office, we went to Alex Sinclair's office. I could tell by his expression that he knew precisely what the conversation with Sir Avery had been. He provided departure information for the morning train.

"I'm to accompanying you as far as the coast."

"Aye," Brodie replied.

"I will bring the necessary travel documents and currency you will need."

He looked from Brodie to me. "I will also provide the name of the cryptographer who can be trusted, should you need to send information."

With that, we left the Tower offices. We rode in silence to the town house rather than the office on the Strand.

"I realize that you tried to get me released from that agreement I made with Sir Avery." I wasn't angry, which surprised me.

The truth was that I was not looking forward to pursing the case further without him. Not, I suppose, that he wanted to hear that. "You don't trust him. After Edinburgh, I understand."

"Sir Avery has loyalty to only one person, the Queen. If he determines that something threatens her or the Crown, he will act as needed."

"Even in the event of a scandal?"

"Most particularly. It's best ye know the way of it. If it came to a choice between the interests of the Crown or ourselves..."

There was no need to explain further.

When we arrived, he had the driver wait and walked me to the entrance of the town house.

With changing seasons, it had grown quite cold on that ride from the Tower as the sun slipped down past the rooflines of the buildings we passed. Misty halos formed around street lamps.

"Mrs. Ryan will have waited supper," I told him, a simple enough invitation. "And there is always my aunt's very fine whisky on a cold evening."

I saw the hesitation and for a moment I thought he would accept.

"Thank ye, no. It is late enough, and there are arrangements to be made."

It was not likely that he meant Mr. Cavendish, or the information he was going to have Dooley follow up about Herr Schmidt's brother-in-law.

"Rory?"

"Aye. I was to take him to the museum."

I could have sworn that he winced.

He had said little about the boy at the office on the Strand

and our travel to Sandringham. There had been other matters of concern.

Since my return, I had paid several visits to Lady Matthews in the aftermath of that very difficult inquiry case.

It did seem that Rory was doing quite well. He had started his studies with a tutor, and now a visit to the London Museum had been planned.

After all the sadness and heartache that she had been through, Adelaide Matthews seemed genuinely happy. And Rory seemed to be doing well.

"The lad seems to have an unnatural curiosity for things, and Lady Matthews thought he might like the museum."

"Lily has become quite fascinated with it," I confided. "Of course, she much prefers the weapons gallery."

He nodded. "She is a *braw* young woman."

"Yes, she is."

"Like yerself."

There was something in his voice, and then gone.

"I try not to overly influence her," I added. "However, with the tales my great-aunt tells her, it may be a losing battle."

"Aye, but she's a smart one. And ye did right bringing her to London."

That had been a mutual arrangement. And now?

We stood there, very much like strangers I thought, trying to find the right things to say after perhaps too many other things had already been said. And I supposed that we were strangers after everything that had happened.

I thought of something I once heard, that once spoken, words could never be taken back. They were always there.

"Mikaela..." He hesitated.

It seemed there was something more he would have said.

Instead, he bid me good evening.

"I will meet you at the rail station in the morning."

I stood at the entrance to the town house and watched as he returned to the cab, tall and lean, dark hair curling over the collar of his coat.

He gave the driver instructions, then climbed inside.

"Well, damn," I softly swore to myself as the cab disappeared down the street.

Nine

WE WERE to meet Alex Sinclair at Charing Cross rail station by ten o'clock for the trip to Dover.

Brodie was already there when I arrived, and Alex joined us shortly after.

He handed us our travel papers as well as an envelope with French currency.

"You'll be traveling as Lady Forsythe," he explained as he handed me my papers. "And as newly married, husband and wife." He glanced uncertainly from me to Brodie.

"Sir Avery thought it would be the best arrangement, so not to raise suspicion. And accommodations have been made for you at the Westminster in Paris. A good many who travel to France stay there, and it is in keeping with the reason you are there, a bit of after-wedding travel."

How considerate of Sir Avery, I thought. I did wonder if he had somehow managed to learn about that ceremony before the magistrate in Scotland.

"It is possible to send a telegram direct from the Westminster. Telephone connections can be problematic. You are to use the code-word Excalibur."

He paused with another nervous glance, first at Brodie who had said nothing until now, and then at me.

"And if there is a difficulty of some sort?"

"Do not contact the local authorities. Sir Avery was most insistent regarding that." He looked at me then.

"If you encounter a difficulty, you are to contact a man by the name of Sancier at the Belleville Gallery. If you should be questioned, you're to tell them that Lady Forsythe is looking to expand her collection," he added with a look at me.

Not that I had a collection. I was familiar with the artist community in Paris from past school days, however, my sister was the art afficionado, not myself. I had a basic education in art. It had never fascinated me as it did my sister, who turned out to be quite talented.

"Has the man, Sancier, been notified?"

"He has, as well as been informed where you will be staying. He will be able to assist if there should be a need," Alex responded. "I trust you have both made arrangements regarding your absence for the next few days so as not to raise questions or cause undo alarm?"

Brodie nodded.

I had placed a telephone call to Sussex Square the previous evening after I arrived back at the town house. In speaking with my great-aunt, I simply explained that I would be working on an inquiry case for a few days with unpredictable hours. I said nothing of setting off for Paris. That would raise too many questions.

"Do give Brodie my regards," she added in spite of the fact that I had not mentioned him. "And do be careful, dear. While the

French are among our ancestors, they can be a bit peevish from time to time. But then you are familiar with that. Do call when you return. Plans are well underway for Lenore and James's wedding."

Once again, it did seem that she was well informed. I had visions of her having her own network of spies about London. And I did wonder if my sister had been informed of the plans.

Alex was to accompany us as far as Dover. The excuse, if anyone inquired, was that he was my brother and was going as far as the coast to send us off. The real reason was to provide assistance if there should be any last-minute issue before boarding the ferry for the cross-channel trip to Dover.

I suspected it had more to do with the fact that Brodie was not at all pleased with being sent off on a matter he was certain Sir Avery's 'people' in France could have handled, and had made no attempt to hide the fact.

"Plausible deniability," he explained as Alex went to check if the train was on time. "If anything should go wrong, Sir Avery will be able to use the excuse that we were simply in the wrong place at the wrong time. And I don't like the fact that he has no hesitation using your title for this."

"Then we simply need to conclude this as quickly as possible, determine what that address might have to do with anything, make our report, and return to London," I pointed out.

"The train is on time. We can proceed to the platform," Alex announced when he returned. "We have a private compartment. For anyone inquiring, I am your brother. I'm accompanying you to the coast to 'see you off on holiday.'"

I smiled to myself. Alex was certainly getting into this. He did need to get away from the office below the Tower more often.

Our train arrived and we settled into our compartment. We

were familiar with the journey from a previous case. Two-and-a-half hours from Dover to Calais and then six hours by train to Paris.

With Alex as our chaperone, there was little conversation, and we arrived at Dover in plenty of time to make the transfer from train to the ferry.

"You're to keep Sir Avery advised of your progress," Alex reminded us again and then bid us farewell.

Of course, I sarcastically thought. In the midst of a case there was more than enough time to write reports and dash off telegrams. The truth was, however, that none of this was Alex's doing. He was merely following orders.

We left the departure area and entered the main area cabin of the ferry. Brodie tucked our bags onto a shelf along with other baggage.

I walked through to the portside deck with seats along the inside wall that were tucked under a shallow overhang to protect against weather. Brodie followed out onto the deck.

The wind had come up across the water, whitecaps appearing out beyond the landing. The crossing would put us in Calais very near evening. Alex had arranged for us to stay at an inn there before continuing on to Paris on a morning train.

Brodie took out his pipe, then filled the bowl. I cupped my hands around it to block the wind as he lit a match. His fingers wrapped around mine the same as dozens of times before, yet different, and I wanted to hold on. For just a moment that dark gaze met mine as he bent his head and took several puffs, then blew out a stream of smoke once the tobacco glowed.

We stood there as the last of the passengers boarded, then filled the cabin of the ferry. Those more adventuresome souls came out onto the deck to take advantage of the sun and fresh air in spite of the sharp wind that whipped from off the water.

The signal that we were departing went out and we steadied ourselves at the railing as mooring lines were cast off and the ferry slowly edged away from the dock. It then turned out into the channel as clouds of steam billowed overhead from the steam engine.

That fragrant pipe smoke wrapped around me like a memory, then disappeared on the wind as I stared out over the water.

"Ye could have refused to be part of the case," he commented and took another draw from the pipe.

"I wanted to be finished with the agreement I made with him." It was as simple as that. After this, I owed nothing to Sir Avery or the Agency.

"That agreement." He tamped out the contents of the pipe at the deck railing, his mouth thinned in a line surrounded by that dark beard. It was the first we had spoken of it.

"The agreement I made to save your life. I would do it again." I turned and went back inside the cabin.

He remained on the deck for the rest of the trip, returning only when darkness fell across the water and the lights from the port of Calais drew closer.

Calais was an ancient seaport used in medieval times for channel crossings. According to my great-aunt, our ancestor had crossed from there into Britain when he set off to conquer everything he came across.

The old part of Calais with its stone and wood beam residences and inns was just beyond the port, while the more modern part of the city that included the rail station spread to the south of the port. *Modern*, of course, meant within the last two to three hundred years.

It was very near nine o'clock in the evening when we disembarked and the last train to Paris had departed earlier.

According to the travel itinerary Alex had provided, we had a reservation for the night at an inn rather than at one of the hotels in the city, and nearer the rail station for our departure in the morning.

Weather that had followed us across the channel had finally set in with a drizzling rain. Brodie found a driver and we made the short ride to the inn.

A boy appeared as soon as we arrived and retrieved our travel bags in a rapid flow of French.

"You are English, *oui*?" he asked as he followed us into the inn. "We have many English guests traveling to Paris."

The inn was typical of older residences found in Calais and other places in France that had been transformed into inns to accommodate travelers from England and other places.

It was built of brick with timber-framed windows and exposed beams in the Norman Style. Shutters on the windows were painted bright blue, with flower boxes glimpsed overhead in the halo of an electric light from second-story window openings as we entered the inn with another couple.

In heavily accented English, the sightly balding man behind the counter informed them that supper could be provided to their room.

"*Oui, monsieur*?" he inquired as Brodie approached the desk and gave the name for our reservation.

"Ah yes, it is here. And supper for you and the lady?'

Neither of us had eaten since leaving London. Brodie nodded and signed the guest register. He was then handed a key.

The same boy who had assisted with our travel bags when we arrived escorted us to our room on the second floor. He deposited the bags near the door, then turned to Brodie with a toothsome grin and was rewarded with a coin. The grin spread even wider.

"I will bring your supper when it is ready," he informed us as he went to the door, undoubtedly in anticipation of another coin.

"He reminds me of Rory," I commented after he left.

They did seem to be of about the same age.

Brodie merely nodded.

He had not spoken of him at length, yet I knew from Adelaide Matthews that he had been a frequent visitor over the past months.

It seemed the boy had become quite attached to him and looked forward to his visits, something that he undoubtedly needed, having never known his father. And then there was that question that still remained.

Was he Rory's father?

It was possible from the brief time he was with Ellie Sutton. I knew that it had weighed heavily on him after her death, that Rory might be orphaned much as he had been at very near the same age.

He lit the fire in the fireplace that had been laid in anticipation of our arrival. I removed my coat and hung it on a hook by the door. The fire quickly caught, and I crossed the room and extended my hands toward the heat.

"It appears the innkeeper is not on the list of establishments that carry her ladyship's whisky," he commented with a gesture to the bottle of wine and two glasses that sat on the table near the hearth.

"You will have to remind Munro," I replied as he went to the table, removed the cork from the bottle, and poured two glasses.

The wine completed what the fire had started, my hands soon warm along with the rest of me.

"Bordeaux," I commented, and at the look from Brodie where he sat across the table added, "The wine."

"Ah, ye know about such things."

"From afternoons when I managed to escape from the school Linnie and I attended in Paris." I took another sip of wine and smiled. "And then there was her determination to visit every gallery in Paris. I was certain that if I had to tour one more museum or art gallery, that I would surely die of boredom."

"Yer misspent youth," he drily commented.

By no means compared to his life on the streets of Edinburgh, but I supposed that was where my adventures first began.

There was a knock on the door. The man at the front desk had arrived with our supper balanced on a tray with a tureen, bowls, and a long twist of bread on a plate.

The boy had accompanied him. He flirted outrageously as he set a second bottle of wine on the table, then expertly opened it.

Everyone in France, it seemed, drank wine, and I had to laugh at that typically French habit and in one so young. Brodie provided father and son each a coin.

The boy thanked Brodie, then turned to me and bowed from the waist.

"*Enchantée, madame.*"

When I would have translated after they left, Brodie nodded as he poured more wine.

"Ye seem to have that effect on most men and boys ye encounter."

And one particular man? I did wonder. Were there still feel-ings there? Was there a way around the angry words, and pain?

The supper was a typical French stew with meat and vegetables in a rich wine sauce, fresh-baked bread that Brodie sliced, and that second bottle of wine.

The hot food drove away the last of the chill from the ride from the Port of Calais, while the wine created a faint glow around everything in the room—including the man who sat across from me with that overlong mane of dark hair. My fingers curled into the palm of my hand.

I pushed back memories as I emptied the last of the wine from my glass, then rose from the table and went to the bed that was only slightly larger than the one at the inn in Norfolk.

I unfastened the button at the waist of my skirt then stepped out of it, then unbuttoned my shirtwaist and shivered in the colder air at the edge of the room, dressed now only in my camisole and long slip. I quickly slipped under the covers on the bed.

He placed more wood on the fire, then returned to the table and emptied the bottle into his glass, legs stretched before him, boots crossed at the ankles as he slowly sipped the wine. And that dark gaze met mine from across the room.

"Ye could have refused to continue with the case."

"I could have. But I wanted to be done with the agreement I made with Sir Avery."

"Aye, the agreement."

I knew his feelings toward Sir Avery. After the case that had taken us both to Edinburgh, he didn't trust him.

"You could have refused as well."

"No," he replied, staring into his glass as he swirled the wine as I had seen him do countless times with a dram of whisky. As if he might find answers there.

"That wasna possible," Brodie replied, that thick Scots accent wrapping around the words.

Why wasn't it possible? I wondered as I drifted in a faint wine haze and closed my eyes.

But the wine, the warmth in the room, and the bed... The question was there, then slipped away with the wine and heat from the fire, and that long trip across the channel.

BRODIE

He rose from the chair then went to the hearth. The fire had burned low once more and the room had grown cold. He put more wood on it, poked at it until it caught and burned brightly, then turned toward the bed.

She was asleep, lips slightly parted, her head resting on one hand on the pillow, the fingers of her other hand wrapped around the edge of the blanket.

He crouched low beside the bed. If he closed his eyes, she was still there, as she had been the past months—the curve of her cheek, the stubborn angle of her chin. Those eyes that were not quite green but not quite gray the way they had been when she had stared back at him in anger that last time.

But when he opened his eyes, she was still there, asleep now, her breathing slow and even, her lips slightly parted with something she might have said.

There was a faint smile, she would want the last comment. She did like to have the last word. Not in anger but something she wanted him to know. To understand?

It had taken all those months apart, countless times that encounter at Scotland Yard had tortured him, and his worst fear had been that he might lose her. In the end he had caused it himself and she had left.

He touched the ring that he had placed on her hand with those few words so many months ago. She still wore it in spite of everything that had passed between them.

Impossible, he had thought, when he told her of his feelings and wanted her for his wife. Impossible for a woman like her and a man like him.

Yet, she had accepted his proposal, had accepted him. And she trusted him. Hadn't she told him so?

That last time, before she left, when he was beaten and chained, she asked him to trust *her*.

He did. It was himself that he didn't trust to be able to keep her safe...if she was out there alone. And the rage that had followed—at Abberline, at himself, and at her!

And now? How did he take away the hurt he saw in her eyes that last time? How did he make her understand that he did trust her? That he needed her there at the office, at the blackboard with her scribbles and her notes, across the desk from him at the end of a day as they shared a dram of whisky. Needed her argument over one reason or another when he was wrong about a clue they'd uncovered, all the other ways that he'd come to know her...needed *her*, when he'd learned not to need anyone.

When he would have returned to the chair before the hearth, her fingers gently closed around his as they had countless times in the past. That simple gesture that had connected them after long days, a frustrating case, and other strong words. It was difficult to know who was holding onto whom.

It didn't matter as he gently eased down onto the bed beside her, then pulled her close.

If she wakened, there were no words, just that quiet way they had found with each other in the past as she stirred and somehow moved closer, then slept once more, trusting him...

Ten

CALAIS TO PARIS

THE COMPARTMENT WAS full as the morning train continued our trip to Paris. Brodie sat across the way.

He had already left the room at the inn when I wakened, dressed, and then joined him in the small dining room of the inn. We ate with only a word or two that passed between us. However, more than once I looked up to find a frown on his face and that dark gaze watching me.

As now, then it was gone as he stared out the window of the compartment, conversations flowing around us in a mixture of French and English.

There were comments about the weather that had set in steadily as we left Calais, the unexpected delay of our departure, a family that had made the crossing from Dover, the mother attempting to soothe her restless young daughter who squirmed.

When would they arrive? What about Titou? Would grand-mère be there?

She eventually ran out of questions, laid her head on her mother's lap, and closed her eyes.

So very simple, I thought, to be a child and the only thought was of a beloved pet or one's grandmother.

We were soon pulling into the Gare du Nord station.

It was a central point of travel in France and beyond, and there were attendants who spoke both French and English. He secured a driver and gave him the address of the hotel where Sir Avery had made reservations for our stay.

I had stayed at the Hotel Westminster at the Rue De La Paix in the past as I returned from one of my trips abroad. It was built by the Duke of Westminster, an acquaintance of my great-aunt, in the style of an English manor house with rich dark woods, marble floors, and fresco ceilings, with suites and rooms in six stories that dominated 13 Rue De La Paix.

A room had been reserved, and Brodie signed the register and inquired about the location of the telegraph office. We were then escorted to our room, smaller and modest in comparison to the suite I had stayed in previously.

Yet there was that familiar expression on Brodie's face. It was much like a tortured prisoner as he glanced at the opulence of the furnishings along with the adjoining bathing chamber, as the attendant poured two glasses of fresh water at the table in the small drawing room.

It was quite a contrast to the inn we had stayed in the night before, or even the townhouse at Mayfair.

"It's said that the Duke of Westminster wanted a place for those traveling to and from England that offered the same amenities as those they were familiar with."

"Did he now? It would seem a bit overdone."

"Somewhat more than Old Lodge," I agreed, thinking of my great-aunt's hunting lodge in the north of Scotland where at least a handful of ancestors had retreated for all sorts of hunting and other somewhat nefarious activities. And where the distillery house was for that very fine whisky.

It was a single-story lodge house with rough-hewn timbers, stone walls and slate floors. Thick wool rugs had been added against cold winters, as well as an enormous fireplace in the main room where some warrior ancestor had undoubtedly stood beside the long table while roast deer was served.

One could almost hear tankards being slammed down on that table to call for more ale, or whisky as it were.

We had gone there after a particularly difficult case. It was there that he had proposed. And it was to Old Lodge I had gone these weeks past, alone.

It was a place that had connected us, two very different people. Perhaps too different? And yet...

It was there the night before, in that inn at Calais. Something that I might have dreamed, but wasn't.

There had been no anger, nothing was said. There was only the sound of the wind as it came up around the inn, the hiss of the fire in the fireplace, and we both slept.

"I'll send off a telegram to let Sir Avery know that we arrived." He went to the door.

"Then we should find the address that was in that note."

13 Rue Miron
The Montparnasse

The hotel provided a driver and Brodie gave him the address I had discovered in the note found among the ashes at Sir Collingwood's residence.

In less than an hour, we had made our way along the edge of central Paris and arrived at the Rue Miron.

Number thirteen was a two-story apartment, in a row of

other apartments built of brick with white plaster over, the number above the wrought iron-framed entrance.

It was an upper middle-class residence at the edge of the district preferred by writers and artists, with small niche art galleries where struggling artists displayed their work. A place my sister had insisted we visit on days when there were no classes.

"The Montparnasse has several art galleries and cafés where writers and artists gather."

"Know it well, do ye?"

"It was an interesting place to visit when I was able to escape with a handful of others from the Lycée St. Germain."

St. Germain was one of a handful of private girls' schools, attended by the daughters in certain English families, that taught more than acceptable social skills necessary for attracting a husband. It was where our great-aunt had attended as a young woman.

There was history regarding her own adventures there during a time of political unrest with the new Republic having established power throughout France, and an incident with a young patriot who had delivered fresh food to the school.

It was a chance encounter in the dining hall of the school when that young Frenchman decided to adorn a wall with an impassioned slogan that was still heard all over France twenty years after the new Republic was established.

In her own words, *"It was a memorable encounter."*

Nothing more was ever said of it.

Yet when I had taken myself off to the Greek Isles after that first trip abroad, she had immediately sent someone to return me to London against any possible indiscretion. Someone with dark hair that hung over his collar, and that dark gaze that met mine now.

"Yer past experiences as a school girl? Escaping with a handful of others?" Brodie commented. "Other reckless young girls, no doubt, with no one about."

"I was fifteen years old that year, very near Lily's age. It was one of my first adventures."

Instead of the comment about it being reckless, foolish in the least, he reached around me and seized the lever of the brass Lionhead door-knocker. When there was no response, he tried again.

"*What are you doing there?*" a voice called out in French from the street.

A woman in the usual dress of a French housekeeper with a shawl around her shoulders, stood on the sidewalk, a shopping basket over her arm.

"We are friends," I replied in French. "We have come to visit."

"Monsieur Dornay is away. He has been gone for several days," she replied, and explained that she worked for the family in an apartment across the street.

She brought fresh fish for him when she went to market. Dornay, she explained gave art lessons to her employer's sons.

I thanked her. She eventually nodded with a curious stare over the shoulder as if I was familiar, then shrugged and continued across the Rue Miron.

An art instructor? And now gone unexpectedly for several days?

Number thirteen Rue Miron had been on that note that someone had burned, obviously with the intention that no one else saw it.

I wondered what we might be able to find inside the apartment. Brodie obviously thought the same.

There was no alleyway or back entrance, only the main entrance at the street.

"Has she returned to her own apartment?" Brodie asked.

"Yes."

"And the street?"

"There is no one about at the moment." Of course, that didn't include anyone who peered out a window of an adjacent apartment.

I could have picked the lock myself. I had become efficient at it, but not nearly as efficient as Brodie. A moment was all that was needed and he had the door open and motioned me inside.

The apartment was typical with the main entrance, a servant's door to one side which undoubtedly led to the kitchen, although there didn't seem to be anyone else about.

There was also small room at the other side that appeared to have been used as a studio for those art lessons the woman had spoken of. Stairs climbed to the second level, where we found a small drawing room with a fireplace, and stairs that led to the third floor with two private rooms.

I had seen such residences, and been inside one that belonged to the family of a student at my school. It had been opulently furnished with carpets, thick drapes on the windows, and furnishings that crowded every room, including a formal dining room.

The apartment at Number Thirteen was quite modest by comparison, with only a minimum of furniture that included a worn settee and overstuffed chair in the drawing room, and a narrow table with chairs for what passed as a dining room in the salon.

The sparse furnishings suggested the owner of the apartment rarely entertained, if at all. And it did seem as if Monsieur

Dornay made only a modest living from lessons he gave. Might that have something to do with the address found on that note? If so, what was the connection?

As we had in the past, we each took a floor of the apartment to search more efficiently for anything that might tell us the reason that address had been on the remnants of that note.

As I climbed the stairs, it did seem odd that the drapes had all been left open. Most people who planned to be away were in the habit of closing their drapes.

There was sufficient light from the windows of the apartment that there was no need to turn on the electric, or use the handheld lamp Brodie usually carried when we made inquiries in a case. It made the search for anything amiss or revealing that much easier.

Brodie had inspected the ground-floor kitchen which revealed there was almost no food in the cold box, and then the small studio on the ground floor. He continued at the second-floor parlor and salon, while I climbed the stairs to the third-floor private rooms.

I entered the first room. The furnishings here were even more sparse and included only a bed and a chair. There was no wardrobe, only hooks along the wall which oddly held a coat, a jacket, several woolen scarves, and an umbrella.

I searched the pockets of the coat and jacket, then around the bed and under the bed, and found nothing. There was no desk or table in this room, therefore little else to search.

A door in the far wall led to a narrow bathroom. Here towels had been left about and there was what seemed a musty smell with no window. A door at the other end very likely connected to that second room on the floor.

What passed for a bathroom, what was called a *salle de*

bain' in France, had a clawfoot tub, badly stained basin, and commode.

Here again, there were a few personal items that included a hairbrush—the sort Brodie used—along with a bottle of hair tonic, and a straight-edged razor. All of which a man would usually take with him for time away.

There was a peculiar musty smell, no doubt due to the towel that lay on the floor where it had obviously been tossed aside. Men, it seemed, according to mentions from my sister when she was previously married or my great-aunt with one of her side comments, were not particularly concerned with such things as hanging up their clothes or a towel after bathing.

Except Brodie, I had discovered. He was quite orderly when it came to his long coat or the few other clothes that he had, no doubt from having few possessions as a boy on the street, nor a roof over his head, as I had learned from Munro.

Brodie was not one to go on about such things. Learning anything about him in the beginning had been like attempting to pry a bone from the hound and frequently had ended with him—Brodie not the hound—simply waving off my question.

"It's not somethin' to concern yerself with," he had told me several times, but it did concern me.

Perhaps now more than ever. With this distance between us I needed to understand. His history, the things that had mattered to him, the good and bad.

I supposed that it was the writer in me, or possibly my own history that drove this need. The past, as I knew only too well, made us who we were.

It became obvious, early in my association with him, that I realized the man he became—honest, true, someone I could trust—was in spite of the horrible years of his youth...*Almost* in spite of them, I thought as I searched the bathroom.

Other than those few personal items and that discarded towel, I found nothing more in the bathroom that might tell me anything and continued through to that adjoining room.

This room had obviously been the artist's private studio where he worked on his own projects when not teaching young students.

Monsieur Dornay obviously preferred to work with oils. There was a shelf on the near wall with tubes of paints, a variety of brushes set on end in a chipped porcelain vase to dry. And the ever-present jar of pungent-smelling liquid—turpentine for cleaning those brushes, as I knew so well from my sister's artistic efforts.

There was a table, hardly in better shape than the one in the dining room below. A vase of withered flowers that might possibly have been a subject for a painting stood on the wooden surface, along with other tools for the artist's work that included several well-used cloths, a square-tipped blade, and a knife. Possibly for creating an effect from particularly thick paint a brush could not achieve, as I had seen my sister do on one of her pieces.

There was also a great deal of trash and rubbish scattered around the room, wadded up artist's paper for drafting subjects before beginning a piece with oils, along with a shattered wine glass and a decanter, the corner of the table stained with the contents.

My sister knew far more about these things that I did, and had explained that artists could be a temperamental lot. It was not unusual for those she had visited, and one in particular who had provided lessons, to explode in a burst of temper at some trivial matter.

Much like a temperamental Scot?

The thought was there and then immediately gone as a memory of the night before returned.

There had been nothing temperamental or angry when I had wakened and Brodie was there beside the bed, his fingers brushing mine. Then the expression on his face as he stared down at my hand in his. Tears had stung in my eyes as I held on and then felt his weight beside me and his warmth surround me. Protecting me?

I took a deep breath and continued my search of the atelier. Amid the smell of paint and turpentine, that smell I experienced in the bathroom was much stronger.

Across the room were several easels of partial and completed works, some draped with canvas. I pulled the canvas back from the nearest one and uncovered a portrait of a young girl with dark hair and blue eyes made all the brilliant by the flowers she held in her hand.

It was a simple painting with only the girl and the sweet expression on her face. But the beauty of it was in the simplicity.

Someone who lived nearby, the daughter of a friend, or perhaps the artist's child?

I had seen nothing else in my search to indicate that a child lived there.

Lowering the canvas back into place, I carefully stepped around other piles of rubbish including a small barrel that had toppled over, and almost tripped over the artist's stool that lay on its side. A body lay alongside it.

I had found the source of that smell, strong, tightening the back of my throat as I clasped a hand to my face.

It's one thing to prepare oneself for the sight at a morgue or funeral, quite another to come upon one unaware and then very nearly step on it.

I heard a muffled sound and I realized that I was the one who made it—startled at my discovery, unprepared for the pool of dried blood that surrounded it, and the ghastly expression on the man's face with eyes wide open.

"What is it? Have ye found something?" Brodie called from the adjacent room, and then he was there.

"Mikaela?"

He found me in that room, then stepped past, going down on one knee beside the body as he had undoubtedly done dozens of times when he was with the MET, and obviously in our private work.

The usual sort of question—Is he dead? Obviously, a moot point. The man was very dead.

"Monsieur Dornay?" I finally recovered enough to say.

"It would seem," Brodie replied. He looked up at me.

"Are ye all right?"

I nodded. "I wasn't expecting a body among the rubbish. Next time, I'll be better prepared." I could have sworn one corner of his mouth curved upward, then quickly disappeared.

"Did ye find anything else?"

I shook my head. "It does seem that there might have been a confrontation in this room."

He looked about, taking in everything in the atelier in a sweeping glance.

"Did you find anything?"

"There was little food in the kitchen. If the woman we saw brought food from market, there was no sign of it. It did seem, however, that someone had eaten in the parlor and there was a half-full bottle of wine."

"A last meal for Monsieur Dornay?"

Brodie shook his head. "There were two plates and two glasses with red color on the rim of one."

A guest? Angeline Cotillard had worn vivid red lip color.

"The same shade we found on that cigarette at Sandringham?"

"It appears so," he replied as he proceeded to search the pockets of the man's vest, the shirt, and then turned him over so that he could search the pockets of his trousers.

I had seen all of this before. Still, a dead body was a gruesome sight even if the person hadn't been stabbed to death, which Monsieur Dornay obviously had.

It was the sound the body made, that release of air from the lungs as the chemist Mr. Brimley had once explained, that could be quite startling. As if the man might simply get to his feet and then carry on a conversation.

Brodie held up a piece of paper.

"You found something?"

He handed it to me then continued his search of the last of the pockets that revealed nothing, then proceeded to remove the artist's boots and search them as well.

"Aye, just as I thought," he announced as he removed a thick roll of currency from one of the boots.

"A considerable amount of money, and all of it is in English notes."

Payment of some sort? For what? One of those paintings? That seemed unlikely based on what I had seen in the room.

Dornay was quite talented, but he was no Rembrandt or Cézanne. Yes, even I knew the difference between. Although that was as far as it went.

What I did know by the condition of the room and the rest of the apartment was that Monsieur Dornay apparently struggled financially as so many artists did. It was difficult to find an audience, much less those who would pay considerable sums for a piece of art.

"The papers I handed ye?"

I unfolded one of them and read the information printed in French. "They're travel papers."

He stood, finished with his search. "For where?"

"Brussels, and there is a handbill for an art exhibit of several French Masters to be given at the Royal Museum there."

"When?"

"The twentieth through the twenty-first."

The twentieth of the month was two days from now. It did seem by those travel papers and the handbill that Dornay had hoped to attend.

We now knew more than when we arrived in Paris, yet I wondered what more we might have learned if Monsieur Dornay was alive.

A sound, muffled and somewhat distant beyond the windows, brought me back to the present and the fact that Brodie and I, who had no right to be here and in fact had more or less broken into a dead man's apartment, were in somewhat of a precarious position that could be difficult to explain.

"It is the *gendarme*."

"The police."

I nodded. It was safe to assume that the housekeeper from across the street had seen us enter the apartment and then notified them. It hardly mattered now. We couldn't risk being found here.

Any explanation would require contact with London, and I knew from experience that could be a lengthy process. The much larger issue was whether or not Sir Avery would even acknowledge that he had sent us, much less provide for our release.

"We canna be found here," Brodie came to the same

conclusion. "Bring the papers. We need to leave before they come up here."

There are some things that are easier said than done.

"There is only the front entrance," I reminded him as sounds came again from the first floor.

That dark gaze went to the large windows at the wall.

"Do you have a plan?" I inquired.

He nodded. "I seem to remember that ye escaped a burning church by way of the roof.

The 'church' was in fact a brothel in Edinburgh where we first met Lily.

I looked at those large windows. "Do you intend for us to escape over the rooftops?"

The next sound brought our attention back to the situation at hand, most definitely the sound of others now inside the apartment on the ground floor.

I looked out onto the slanted roof of the apartment building behind the one at Number Thirteen. The building I now stared at was no more than three stories tall and that slanted roof was twenty or more feet below.

"How do you propose that we...?" I got no further with the question as I turned around.

Brodie had pulled most of the canvas and several drop cloths from Dornay's paintings and was presently tying them together end-to-end. He looked up.

"Unless ye wish to await the police and explain the situation to them."

I gave him a look he was most familiar with.

"Aye, ye might grab the cloth from that painting."

I didn't care to wait for the French police. They seemed to have a particular dislike for English citizens in spite of the travelers that passed through and spent a great deal of money here.

We had been warned about that dislike years before at the school my sister and I attended.

I seized the nearest drop cloth and pulled it from the painting it covered to reveal a nude painting in progress.

There was enough 'in progress' to make out all the intimate parts as the model reclined on a settee. She was quite robust with long blonde hair that draped around her ample parts.

Brodie appeared with that trail of canvas and linen in hand. He handed me one end of the canvas rope he'd made.

"Come along now unless ye wish to greet the police at the door."

He climbed up onto the wide window casement as if it was something he did every day and I was reminded that he hadn't always been with the police. He held out his hand and pulled me up beside him.

He tied one of the *'ropes'* he had made to the iron frame of the window, then tested his weight against it. With a nod, he turned and then dropped the loop that he tied at the long end over my head and then under my arms as he explained that he was going to lower me to that roof below, then follow.

"Yer not going to argue about it?"

More sounds came from inside the apartment, much closer now.

"Perhaps when we have more time," I replied.

He shook his head, then held onto me as I climbed out the window. He slowly lowered me to the adjacent rooftop. But instead of pulling it back up, he climbed out onto the narrow ledge, then quickly lowered himself down beside me.

"You have done this before," I commented.

"Perhaps," he replied.

He immediately crossed the roof to the front of the building, then returned across the narrow edge of that slanted roof, much like a cat in spite of his height. Of course, he was not that tall as a lad in Edinburgh and then London.

Cat burglar, I thought.

"Watch yer footing," he cautioned as he took hold of my gloved hand and we crossed the roof together, like two cats.

There was a drainpipe for the runoff of rain on the near corner. It ran down the side of the building to the street below.

"The pipe runs past the balcony at the apartment below, then down to the street." He took hold of the pipe with both hands. "It should hold."

"Wait..." I cautioned. "I'm fairly certain that I weigh less. Perhaps I should go first, to test it."

That dark gaze met mine. "If it holds me, it will be safe for ye."

And with that, he began the climb down.

Bloody stubborn man, I thought. Secured by metal brackets, the pipe held as he descended to that balcony, hand over hand. He reached the edge of the balcony, climbed over the railing, then looked up.

A cat, indeed!

I had climbed trees in Scotland and at Sussex Square as a child, usually successfully, and on occasion in my work with Brodie. That hot air balloon came to mind along with the 'church' in Edinburgh.

However, never down a drainpipe with the French police undoubtedly about to enter that top floor atelier and discover Monsieur Dornay's body.

I took hold of the pipe as Brodie had, grateful that I had worn gloves, and began that descent, and silently cursed women's fashion even with the split skirt I was wearing along the way.

I found a toe-hold on the bracket below the one at the

roofline as he had, held on and lowered myself until I reached the next bracket, and the next until I felt a strong grip on one leg then at my waist.

I was lifted over the railing of the balcony and let go of the pipe. He pulled me to him, arm around my waist, his other hand clasping my head.

My hair had come undone in our escape from the other apartment. There was that dark gaze, myself quite breathless from the dangerous climb down the drainpipe, the length of him pressed against me.

And I thought it was very possible that Michaelangelo's statue of David, considered quite risqué, had nothing over Angus Brodie.

Eleven

OUR ESCAPE WAS SIMPLY DONE. There was no one home in the apartment with that balcony.

Brodie handily picked the lock on the glass doors. We let ourselves in, then let ourselves out on the street below in front of a tobacconist's shop. Then we walked several streets past until we found a driver of one of hundreds of *fiacres* that provided transportation across the city.

We left the district at the river, however, the driver explained that his license did not allow him to cross into other areas.

The promise of a hundred francs to take us across, then to the Westminster convinced him. Not surprisingly, he hung a cloth with another number on it over the one painted on the side of his carriage, and we continued across the river.

It was late in the afternoon when we arrived at the Westminster, the sun a fiery orange glow below the bank of clouds that had pulled back from the river.

I was tired with at least a half dozen bruises that I could feel from climbing down from rooftops. Our clothes were somewhat disheveled although I had attempted to restore some order to my hair, while Brodie looked much the same as I had often seen him when on a case about London. I thought of the trousers I had borrowed in our previous case.

It was a reminder that I did need to consider having some made that fit better than a man's trousers. That thought had momentarily stopped all others—that I considered I might have a need for them.

Which of course then led to the next thought about my relationship with the man beside me in that carriage.

Our driver was well paid when we arrived at the Westminster.

"Go to the room," Brodie told me as we entered the hotel. "I need to send a message to London."

I nodded. I was too tired to argue.

"Excalibur," I reminded him of the code-name Alex Sinclair said we were to use before we left London.

It did all seem quite nefarious, I thought.

A member of the Admiralty brutally murdered, a name scribbled on that message found in Sir Collingwood's fireplace, a struggling artist murdered at the apartment at Number Thirteen Rue Miron, those travel papers and the handbill for that exhibition at the museum in Brussels, along with a code name we were supposed to use?

What did all of it mean? What had we stumbled into?

I had visited the Westminster when our great-aunt visited my sister and me at school in Paris, and I was familiar with the hotel. While Brodie went to send off that telegram, I passed by the men's sitting room, an elegant recreation of a gentlemen's club.

I entered the room and was immediately informed by an attendant that the club was for gentlemen only. I thanked him and continued to the mahogany bar where I requested not wine but whisky, preferably Old Lodge whisky imported from Scotland.

To my surprise they carried a bottle of my great-aunt's whisky. Bless Munro who handled that enterprise, I thought, then inquired about supper.

The man behind the bar informed me with a familiar English accent that there were a variety of entrees provided for the guests of the men's sitting room.

I placed an order for supper and a bottle of whisky, gave the man the room number for the meal to be delivered, then tucked that bottle into my bag and ignored the stares of the gentlemen who were present as I left.

In spite of the fact that we had one of the smaller rooms in the hotel, it did have a gas fireplace. I soon had a fire going, opened that bottle of whisky, poured two glasses, and then took out my notebook.

Brodie arrived soon after. He looked tired with faint lines around those dark eyes and his mouth. He pulled his revolver from his pocket and set it on the table. I handed him that other glass of whisky.

"I suppose ye pulled this from yer bag," he commented after taking a very long taste.

"It seems that Munro has invaded the Continent with my aunt's whisky," I replied.

"A good man," he replied, as he went to one of those fine satin brocade-covered chairs before the fire, sat, drained the tumbler, and then held it out for another dram. He immediately took another long drink as I handed it back to him.

"I explained wot we found as best I could in a brief message." He leaned his head on the chair back, eyes closed as he let the whisky have its way.

"Ye can send the next message. I have no idea if I spelled those French words or that damned code word correctly."

It was a small thing, but it was a reminder that we worked very well together, all things considered, including spelling.

Was that all that was left?

I had made my notes regarding our discoveries of the day and set my pen aside. I then went into the adjacent bathroom and turned on the tap to fill the bathtub with hot water.

I slowly undressed, stepped out of my clothes, and discovered those bruises. They were quite vivid in shades of blue. I stepped into the tub and slowly sank down into the hot water.

Not usually one for extravagance—after all I had bathed in rivers and from a bucket when on my travels—there was still something I very much appreciated about the fragrant milled soap, the creamy lather it provided, and that extra dram of my aunt's very fine whisky.

I had woven my hair into a single braid after I'd lost the pins while climbing out of that apartment building. I leaned back and closed my eyes, hot water and that soap working another bit of magic.

I drifted in a sea of soap, warm water, steam, and whisky, my muscles slowly loosening. The thought occurred to me that I might have drowned, and didn't care.

Except that I was still breathing, there was a murder case to be solved, and there was a very dark gaze watching me through that steamy, whisky-laden haze.

Brodie leaned over the tub. With anyone else I would have been embarrassed at the least, angry at best. But this was Brodie and I did suppose that we were past embarrassment in consideration of the fact that we were husband and wife, as he had clearly informed the man at the inn in Calais.

"A man has arrived with what appears to be supper, unless

ye've a mind to remain until the water is cold or ye begin to take on the look of a prune."

There were few things that would have pulled me from a warm bath after escaping buildings in Paris. Food was one of them—I was starving. The other thing...

When I would have reached for the towel, an enormous, soft extravagant thing with a large 'W' stitched into one corner, Brodie grabbed it then wrapped it around me.

"Ye'll catch yer death." He then began to dry me off from head to foot.

"Ye've some fine bruises there," he said as his ministrations traveled down one leg then the other.

"A caution regarding climbing out of three-story windows," I replied, not at all put off by his attention as he proceeded to dry off my other leg, his mouth curving down in a frown.

He stood and wrapped the towel, that reached from neck to foot like a blanket, around me.

"I suppose that will do."

It would have to, I thought, as I returned to the bedroom. The attendant who brought the food had set out silverware, damask napkins, and included two covered plates. The aroma that filled the room was quite wonderful.

"Escargot!" I exclaimed as I uncovered one of the serving dishes. "I was quite famished."

"Snails," Brodie added with disgust.

"I ordered them for myself," I informed him as he poured more whisky.

In deference to his simpler tastes, in addition to the escargot for myself, I had ordered beef Bourguignon, or as he preferred to call it, beef stew, with fresh croissants.

We ate in silence until the food had started to warm my
stomach. Or it might have been the whisky.

"Was there any trouble sending the telegram?" I buttered
another croissant and took a bite.

"I waited to see if there would be a response. It seems there
has been development regarding Sir Collingwood and perhaps
the reason he was murdered."

"Did he say what that was?"

He shook his head. "His reply was very cryptic. He
mentioned only that there was a development. Based on what
we discovered, he wants us to continue to Brussels to attend
that exhibition. He'll be sending more instructions at that
time. He didn't want to explain in a telegram."

Most interesting. However, while there were instructions,
there was obviously a great deal that had been left unspoken.
Even in my somewhat hazy condition, it was obvious that Sir
Avery was taking additional precautions regarding information
that was sent back and forth.

"Are ye still hungry, lass?"

I caught that last part, even in the glow of my aunt's
whisky. Then there was the way his voice softened and the
sound of a faint smile when he asked if I was still hungry.

"Ye have an appetite like no other," he teased.

"It's due to climbing out of buildings."

"Which ye are quite good at," he added. "Except, perhaps,
for the bruises."

I held out my empty glass. "More, please."

He poured more for both of us, with a critical glance at the
bottle that now contained substantially less than before supper,
then handed my glass back to me. I gathered my towel about
me and went to the fireplace where it was warmer. And he was
there.

He lifted my hair from my shoulder as he had dozens of times in the past before...

"Yer hair is still damp from yer bath." He removed the tie from the end.

When I didn't protest, he slowly began to unwind the braid, and I watched as those fingers gently tugged, until my hair was loose about my shoulders and he fanned it before the heat of the fire.

I blamed it on the whisky, of course, or it might have been the escargot. Or quite simply it could have been the man whose hands rested gently on my shoulders as he turned me toward him.

His hands skimmed my throat, then his mouth found mine. The taste of whisky was there, along with that faint scent of cinnamon and orange as he kissed me on one corner of my mouth then the other.

Inexplicably, I thought of my great-aunt and a conversation when we were on safari, a night with the restless sounds of a pride of lions beyond the compound where we stayed.

"The females hunt and the males...do what males do, and protect the pride," Sir Ellery, our host, had explained, as we sat before our tent, the sun slowly going down in a spectacular way.

"All that roaring about," my great-aunt replied over a glass of her whisky that she had sent on ahead of our trip there, and a look over at me.

"Not unlike the human male. They bicker and quarrel, and somehow continue on..."

I had said nothing to her about the reason for my last-minute decision to accompany her and Lily to Africa. Even so, there it was. Greater wisdom over a bit of the drink?

It *was* the whisky, I told myself as I struggled to breathe and he whispered in Gaelic. Words I had no idea the meaning of that slipped through the haze as his mouth found mine once more. And in spite of everything, that lion roar and harsh words that had pushed me away...I wanted more.

His beard tickled my neck as he tugged my head back, and his lips followed, teeth nipping, demanding, then giving, and I was certain that the French in this regard were highly overrated.

The kiss ended and we were both breathless, and the look in that dark gaze...as he took my hand and kissed the back of my fingers, just there at the ring I still wore.

"Will ye come to bed with me?" he whispered.

I knew what that meant after what had just passed between us.

The answer was there, I suppose where it began on a beach on the Isle of Crete with the hot sun beating down, in the north of Scotland with those simple words spoken before a magistrate, and even with the anger that had driven us apart.

He pushed the towel back from my shoulders. It dropped to the floor, and for just a moment I thought of that painting in Dornay's atelier, the woman naked, reclined back against that chaise.

He picked me up and carried me to the bed.

It was the whisky, I told myself as my toes curled.

Sometime later, he retrieved the satin brocade quilt that had somehow ended up on the floor and pulled it over us, then wrapped his arm around me and pulled me against him. His hand moved over mine, his fingers brushing the ring on my hand. And there in the darkness, the 'lion's roar' was gone.

"I know that I hurt ye. It was never my intent."

I felt the deep breath he took against my back.

"When I told ye that I didna want ye to be part of the case, after what Abberline did and knowin' the man, what he was capable of," his voice trailed off, but when I would have said something, his fingers gently closed around mine, stopping me.

"Let me say it," he whispered, and then was quiet for several moments. Gathering his thoughts?

"Ye were like a gift in my life, something good and true, something a man like me...and what happened all those years before..."

I heard that sudden huskiness in his throat and knew he remembered that loss when he was no older than Rory.

"My worst fear..." he whispered, "was that I might lose ye. There are things I've done, things I can bear," he added. "But never that."

He spoke of Rory then. "I thought, too, of him. And Lily, as well, in that dark cell. The commitment the both of us made, to be a family. If something was to happen to ye and with me facing the hangman's rope, what would happen to them?"

It was the first time we had spoken of it after that horrible argument, and something quite extraordinary in a man, particularly a Scot, who was not accustomed to such things.

I fell the brush of his beard against the back of my shoulder as he pressed a kiss there.

"Ye are the strongest, bravest person, man or woman, I've ever known. Ye have a strength inside ye that few men have. With what Abberline had already done, I couldna bear the thought that he might hurt ye...Or worse, and there would be nothing I could do to stop him."

I turned and laid my hand against his cheek, my fingers stroking through the soft beard there.

"You should have trusted me."

"Aye."

We were both quiet for a long time, but neither of us slept as I thought of what he'd said.

I took a deep breath. "When I was nine years old, my father took his own life and I saw it afterward."

He knew that much. But I had never spoken of what I felt, finding him in the stables, and all that blood.

"He was quite handsome and strong, and the center of our world after our mother's illnesses. And then he wasn't. He was always gone with his friends, often for days at a time.

"It was only afterward...that I heard the whispers about the women and the gambling debts that eventually took everything we had. His excesses would have put us on the street if not for our great-aunt.

"All I remembered of that time were his absences, the arguments that I didn't understand. But I understood the pain he caused my mother as he kept things from her. I always suspected that she heard the rumors and the gossip as well. Then, she was so very ill, and then she was gone."

I took a deep breath as I shared what I had never shared with anyone, not my sister nor our great-aunt, as much as loved them both. Perhaps *because* I loved them.

"When you told me you didn't want me to be part of case, and you were so very angry, I was terrified what Abberline would do, and determined that I had to find Ellie Sutton's murderer to prove you were innocent. All I wanted was for you to be safe."

"And I pushed ye away." He took my hand and kissed my fingers. "Strong, stubborn, someone to trust with my life." Then, "Are ye certain there is no Scot's blood in ye?"

It was an attempt, I knew, to ease the moment between us. To say what needed to be said and then, as my great-aunt would say, '*get on with it.*'

"There might be a smuggler or a highwayman or two," I replied and wiped away a tear.

"Aye, criminals to be certain." He paused.

I sensed there was more that needed to be said.

"Ye tore my heart out when ye left, with just that note, and I knew that I had hurt ye in a way that ye might not forgive." He held my hand in his and kissed it.

"My greatest fear was losing ye, and I'd done it to myself."

I turned so that I lay facing him. I curved my hand against his cheek, my fingers stroking through that dark beard, that dark gaze finding mine.

"There are those who canna be trusted," he continued, his hand over mine. "They dinna try to hide who and what they are. Then, there are others who hide behind words, but ye learn who they really are, sometimes the hard way.

I knew he spoke of Abberline once again.

"I do trust ye, lass. It's others that canna be trusted. And if they were to harm ye...I will always protect ye. I canna change that."

The rest of it went unspoken, but I knew what he meant and I shivered at the thought of what he was saying.

"Ye are a part of me." He tipped my chin up. "I love ye. God knows, ye are a troublesome baggage, but I do and that's the way of it, Mikaela Forsythe Brodie."

Twelve

I WAS NOT foolish enough to think that all of our issues had been resolved. We were very different people, who had come from different places.

Yet, at the heart of it all, in what truly mattered, we were very much the same.

We spoke of other things in the hours afterward until the gray light of morning crept around the edge of the drapes at the windows.

"Do ye want to continue?"

I suppose that was his way of showing that he trusted my judgment, and trusted me. It was something quite new between us.

I assured him that I wanted to see the matter done, so that the agreement I had made was fulfilled and done with.

It was obvious that he considered Sir Avery to be somewhat of the same consideration as Abberline. There were things he kept hidden and that obviously troubled Brodie.

As for himself?

"It is a partnership," I reminded him as I dressed in the morning. "What do you want to do?"

Early upon rising, admittedly with little sleep, I did check my toes with some amusement and they seemed intact. I had handed my notebook to him, to go over my notes in case I had forgotten anything when I made my latest entries the previous evening.

"We will see it through," he replied, but I heard the caution in his voice.

"You don't trust Sir Avery?" And with good reason, I thought, after that previous case that took us both to Edinburgh.

Brodie leaned over as I sat before the dressing table, brushing my hair before pinning it back. He gathered a handful and stroked it with his fingers.

"I am hopeful that we will have other information as well. Perhaps from Alex."

I looked up at his reflection in the mirror.

"You sent him a telegram as well?"

"Aye. Sir Avery is the sort who keeps things hidden. And that can be even more dangerous."

I understood his meaning and knew from the previous evening that Sir Avery wanted us to continue on to Brussels after the information we found at Monsieur Dornay's apartment.

There, we were to attend the latest art exhibition that was opening at the Royal Museum, according to that handbill we found at the apartment along with Dornay's travel papers.

He had obviously intended to see the exhibit, although we had no way of knowing as yet what that meant as far as Sir Collingwood's murder.

And now, Sir Avery had decided to send Alex Sinclair over with new information. It was obvious that he didn't trust the information to a telegram. We were to meet Alex in Brussels at the Hotel Castelan. I could only wonder what the information might be, so highly confidential that it was to be hand-delivered.

"We will need to make our travel arrangements," I commented as Brodie went to the door. "The hotel concierge can do that for us."

"The fewer people who know our destination perhaps the better. We should make the arrangements ourselves."

I did understand his meaning. Two people were dead. The two murders were somehow connected, but we had no way of knowing how. Not yet.

We agreed to meet downstairs at the restaurant that was open early to accommodate travelers eager to get on their way.

Brodie had already packed his few clothes into the leather valise he had brought with him. I carefully folded my clothes from the day before, then put them into my carpet bag along with personal things, and my notebook.

I had dressed for travel once more in a long skirt, shirtwaist, jacket, and boots. I slipped the knife Munro had given me down the outside of my right boot, then seized my umbrella and gloves. The gloves had been a necessity the day before. After all, one never knew when one might have to escape from a building.

At the restaurant I ordered breakfast for both of us along with coffee—black, and very strong. Brodie arrived just as the meals were being served.

"Any news?" I inquired.

"Alex left this morning for Dover. He is to travel direct from Calais to Brussels," he added in a quiet manner. "He should arrive in Brussels by early evening, and will meet us at the hotel."

"I asked the concierge for a rail schedule." Not an unusual request for travelers. "There is a train departing Gare de Nord for the north, including Brussels, three times daily. The next train today departs at twelve noon, and arrives just before five o'clock. I brought both of our bags. All that is needed is for us to sign out with the desk clerk."

He shook his head. "We will simply leave, as though for the day as other travelers. There is no need for anyone know that we have left the city."

"Do you believe that we are being followed?"

"It is safe to assume that whoever killed the artist may have also seen those travel papers and the handbill. The man had not been dead long. The blood from his wounds was still bright red."

I had noticed, but didn't know what that might mean, other than the fact that he was very dead.

"It is possible that he was interrupted by our arrival and would have returned, and also verra possible that he was watching the building, and then the police arrived."

Observations from years with the MET. I did see his meaning. Brodie stood and assisted with my chair.

"I am not an invalid," I pointed out.

"Ye certainly are not an invalid, but ye are my wife."

Even after our conversations through the night, and then this morning, I sensed the question, perhaps doubt that still remained.

During that conversation that drifted away then returned in the small hours of the morning, he spoke of having met with Sir Laughton, my great-aunt's lawyer, who had been instrumental along with Sir Avery in getting Brodie released from Abberline's custody in the previous investigation.

He had inquired how the marriage might be undone if one of us chose to do so. As it had taken place before the magistrate in Inveresk, in Scotland, it could be done by bringing a petition before a judge who would then simply nullify the marriage.

I was stunned that he had gone so far as to inquire...

"If ye wanted it undone, I would not stand in yer way," Brodie had then said as streaks of gray light slanted into the room from the balcony.

"But no words from a judge could undo what I promised ye, or ye to me."

Bloody stubborn Scot, I thought at the time. Yet I knew that he was right.

While I hadn't known how there could possibly be a way forward for us with all that anger and pain between us, I did know that there would never be anyone that I would give myself to as I had Angus Brodie—a man who was intelligent, handsome, honest and true...a man I could trust.

"I'll leave before ye, and wait for ye across from the hotel," he told me now. "Then ye follow as if yer off to do yer shopping."

"We'll need a carriage."

"We'll find one away from the hotel," he replied. "So that we can be certain we are not followed."

"Our travel bags?"

"Ye always have yours with ye, so it should not draw any attention. I will simply be discreet."

Discreet? Over six feet tall, a handsome figure of a man— particularly in the suit that fit perfectly over that white shirt that any gentleman at the Westminster might wear—and then the contrast of that overlong dark hair and the dark beard...

I watched as he approached the desk, made an inquiry, nodded, then left the hotel. I waited a suitable amount of time, finished my coffee, then also left.

He was waiting outside a flower shop across from the hotel.

I was curious. "What did you say to the desk clerk?"

"I inquired if there is a tonsorial parlor near."

I looked over at him as we departed in the direction I was most familiar with near the Westminster.

"What is that look I'm seein' on yer face?"

"Tonsorial parlor?" I repeated.

"Where a man might get a haircut and a shave," Brodie replied.

"And something more in the room behind the front of the shop?" I casually mentioned what I had heard of in the past.

I could tell by the expression on his face that he knew exactly what I was talking about.

"Perhaps a shine for a man's boots," he suggested with just a slight curve at one corner of his mouth.

Shine his boots? Indeed.

Our conversation had returned to that easy exchange we had often shared, but there was a difference now. Perhaps due to that conversation the night before.

Admittedly we were different after that argument and our time apart. But now we were together again with that banter we had always shared and the exchange of thoughts and ideas.

I had no illusion that someone who had been through what he had and with that strong Scottish identity was now a changed man. He had said as much, that he would always protect me, in spite of myself.

I had lived the past twenty years of my life determined that I could protect myself, and my sister if need be. I told myself that I didn't need anyone else. Yet, these past months apart, I had learned that it wasn't so much that I needed Brodie. I wanted to be with him. Married or not.

Scandalous as that thought might be, I didn't give a fig. I wanted the arguments over an inquiry case, that exchange of ideas that no other man had ever considered I could provide.

I wanted the quiet moments after at the office on the Strand over my aunt's very fine whisky, and when he slowly loosened the braid from my hair, then took my hand, and...

We found a driver very near the Westminster and gave him instructions to take us to Paris Nord station. We arrived in good time to purchase our travel vouchers.

The next train was to leave for Brussels in less than an hour. We then made our way to the platform for the north-bound train.

Very near the platform, I stopped and looked back over my shoulder once more, searching the passengers who had arrived and, like ourselves, were soon to depart.

"What is it?"

"I thought I saw someone that I recognized." Although I wasn't certain.

"Man or woman?"

"I'm not certain." I know that sounded ridiculous.

"It was just a glimpse, and with so many people about..."

He looked past me, searching the faces of those who now crowded the platform as our train arrived and passengers departed. I looked back once more at the faces of people around us, but whatever or whomever I thought I had seen wasn't there.

"I must have been mistaken."

We boarded the train and found our compartment.

I had taken the Nord express from Paris on an adventure trip, on a route that had taken me to Munich, Vienna,

Budapest, then Istanbul. On the return we had taken a more northerly train route that had stopped briefly in Brussels before returning to Paris.

I could not say that I was familiar with all of Brussels, yet my travel companion at the time and I had spent three days there.

When in Brussels...

My great-aunt was familiar with the city and had provided a list of places that I absolutely must see. And then there was chocolate, Belgian chocolate to be precise, unlike anywhere else in the world.

My great-aunt had provided the name of a shop we were to visit in order to bring back the finest chocolate. Jean Neuhaus and his wife, with their shop in the Galerie de La Reine.

It had been somewhat disconcerting when we entered the shop and discovered that Monsieur Neuhaus was quite familiar with the 'English Lady Antonia Montgomery.'

My great-aunt had property in France where she used to travel frequently. Until that adventure trip, I was not aware of her wanderings into Belgium, and beyond.

"I was once young like yourself," she had told me. *"The difference is that when I traveled then, it was often necessary to travel dressed as a man. For protection you see. It did account for some very interesting encounters. And monsieur's chocolate? Exquisite.*

"It does have aphrodisiac qualities, you know."

Actually, more than I wanted to know at the age of seventeen years at the time, as I shared the story with Brodie.

"Aphrodisiac?" he repeated with a lift of that dark brow with the scar through it as we sat across from each other in our train compartment for the trip that would take between four and five hours.

He did resemble some dark, mysterious, nefarious character with that one look. It was apparent he knew the meaning of the word.

It was late in the afternoon when we arrived in Brussels. It was almost another full hour before we were able to find a driver to take us to the Hotel Castelan very near the center of the city where we were to meet with Alex Sinclair, and very near another hour through late afternoon traffic on the street before we arrived.

Brodie paid the driver, with some exchange of conversation. It seemed the driver attempted to take advantage and charge almost twice the fare quoted when we left the train station.

It was amusing to watch. I almost felt sympathy for the driver as he couldn't possibly know that he was quibbling with a man whose people were known for being frugal and a former police detective as well.

I could have intervened, but I was curious to see who would win the difference of opinion. In the end the driver acknowledged the fare he had quoted, arguing that he was losing additional fares arguing over the matter.

"What was the last of it?" Brodie asked after the driver made a comment in French, along with a gesture.

I waited until he was well away before sharing that bit of information. The gesture needed no explanation.

"He welcomed us to the city and hoped that our stay would be a pleasant one."

"Ye are a magnificent liar, Mikaela Forsythe Brodie."

"Only when absolutely necessary."

There was something in his voice, soft and low at my name that was now part of his. At the same time, my throat tightened. I did very much like the sound of it as if I was now complete somehow, connected to this man whom I respected, trusted, and *loved*. In a way that I had thought never possible.

The word came so easily. Not to say that we didn't have our differences, perhaps would always have them, but there was the feeling that we had confronted something and come out of it with something that was deeper, truer, and as he told me when we exchanged those few words in Scotland...forever.

The information Brodie had received from London indicated that we had accommodations at the hotel.

It was also where we were to meet with Alex Sinclair, who was hand-carrying a dispatch from Sir Avery with new information he'd been able to learn regarding Sir Collingwood's murder.

The Castelan was a four-story former private residence, built in the seventeenth century, that included other private residences along the Rue Neuve at the edge of the city center, and only a short distance from the Royal Museum and that exhibition of fine art which was to open the following day.

The main entrance might have been the entrance to the apartments of a titled nobleman, the front desk to greet arrivals on one wall of the main foyer with a staircase that rose to the floors above, and a ground floor salon that had been transformed into a dining room for guests.

We were informed that *Monsieur Sinclair* had not yet arrived and were then shown to our room. The attendant handed Brodie the key and informed us that the dining room would open at seven that evening.

The room was in the style of the private bedroom that it had once been with an entrance to the small sitting room with a fireplace, and an 'accommodation,' as it was called, off the adjacent bedroom.

When I returned, Brodie asked if I would like to accompany him with a tour of the hotel.

"Bring yer notebook," he told me as I followed him from our room. He stopped just outside the doorway.

"Tear off a bit of paper from yer notebook."

I handed him the piece of paper and then watched with growing curiosity as he inserted it inside the edge of the door as he closed and then locked it.

"If anyone should enter the room before we return," he explained.

It was so simple and quite ingenious.

"I suppose you learned that in service with the MET, or on the streets as a boy." I was quite impressed.

"I'm not of a mind of escaping through the window from the third floor."

He did have a point.

Our 'tour' included the fourth floor where we discovered a door with a short stairway that led up to the roof. We then toured the second floor, then down to the ground floor.

In addition to the foyer and the adjacent dining room, there was a flower shop beside the main entrance that fronted onto the street and a door in the hallway opposite the street.

It was discreetly marked—*Personnel Seulement.*

I nodded toward that door, then stepped inside the flower shop as a distraction if anyone should be watching as Brodie waited until the front desk attendant was occupied with another guest, then quickly stepped inside and closed the door behind him.

He was gone for several moments, then just as quickly reappeared, closing the door after him.

"It appears to be the laundry room for this hotel and the

Thirteen

I PICKED up the subtle nod between the two longtime friends. Some sort of silent message that passed between them.

"Mr. Munro," Brodie acknowledged. "Good of ye to join us."

There was then a greeting to Alex Sinclair, as if the two men simply joined us for supper.

Alex continued the charade. "It has been some time, Mr. and Mrs. Brodie."

Friends greeting friends. Obviously for the benefit of others in the dining room. Some had looked up, but others simply continued on with their meal.

"Have you eaten?" I inquired of them, playing my part.

"Not yet," Alex replied. "Business to attend to."

Business that I was most anxious to hear about.

A waiter appeared and recited the evening's dinner fare. Munro gave his order, as any gentleman might.

I had known him for several years as my great-aunt's manager of her estates. He was most usually a man of few words. But I was aware that, like Brodie, he watched everyone and everything about him.

No doubt, very much like Brodie, things learned on the streets as young boys, both without family and left to survive on their own. And, like Brodie, very much a Scot.

However, I was very aware that, also like Brodie, there was that other side to the man. That side of him that had insured a young woman traveling on her own was capable of protecting herself.

He had given me the blade that folded several years before, along with lessons on how to use it. I had practiced the moves he taught me for weeks before departing.

"I have perhaps taught her too well. I pity the person she encounters," he had announced.

At which my great-aunt replied, *"Excellent. Well done. I shall worry only a little about her."*

And I had set off in the company of others from England, quite safe...there was that little side adventure I had undertaken to the Isle of Crete with our travel guide, where I had encountered another Scot.

Although at the time, I had been too peeved that my great-aunt had sent someone to 'retrieve' me before I came to some harm at the hands of that particularly handsome, young Greek guide.

At the time I saw no harm in swimming in the Aegean *'en flagrant,'* away from the prying gazes of my travel companions. And there had been that brooding, dark gaze of the man sent to rescue me and accompany me back to London.

I was somewhat younger at the time and chose to ignore the man as much as possible on that return trip.

It became the plot for my first novel with my protagonist, Emma Fortescue, which had scandalized polite society in

London. But the ladies of London were discovered reading it and the novels that followed about Miss Fortescue's adventures, while concealing them inside the latest daily newspaper.

And that, as they say, was the beginning of several more adventures to follow, including the man now sitting across from me.

We continued the charade and passed the next hour in companionable conversation about anything and everything trivial with our 'guests.'

Then, as it grew later, many of the guests in the dining room departed. I rose from the table and, in a performance that would have rivaled that of my good friend, Templeton, announced for the benefit of those who were left in the dining room and any others, that I was 'quite tired as it had been a long day.'

"Of course." Brodie stood. "I will escort you."

It took some effort not to smile at that one. Escort me?

I did suspect that it was all part of the 'performance.' It was entirely possible that he was taking precautions which I didn't understand in the moment. I then watched as he turned to Munro who was seated to his right.

He extended his hand as anyone might do in parting. Munro stood and did likewise, then took Brodie's hand in a gentlemanly gesture for an extended handshake.

Brodie concluded by informing our 'guests' that we would see them in the morning. We then departed the dining room.

The hotel manager at the front counter nodded and in heavily accented English bid us good evening. We proceeded to our room.

Once there, Brodie inserted the key into the lock then slowly opened the door. The piece of paper that he'd inserted earlier at the edge of the door dropped to the floor. It did appear that no one had been in our room while we were away.

"What is to be done now?"

It was obvious that it was important we learn the information that Alex had brought with him from London. And there was the added curiosity about Munro's appearance.

"We wait."

"For?"

"For them to join us."

"But how will they know...?"

He took my hand in a gesture as if to shake it. And then, tapped the palm of my hand in a way that no one would have seen, except if they knew to look for it.

Twice, then four times. Two and four. Our room number, 204!

Very shortly, there was a subtle knock at the door, that same code, twice then four times.

Brodie went to the door. "Ye checked the hallway?" I heard him ask.

"Aye."

And we were joined in the room by Munro and Alex Sinclair. Munro carried a wrapped parcel that he set on the table before the fireplace.

"Ingenious," Alex declared. "I would never have guessed..."

Brodie motioned him to silence, checked the hallway once more, then closed the door and set the lock.

"Wot are ye doin' here?" he demanded of Munro. "The telegram spoke only of Alex."

Munro nodded. "I acquired information that I thought might be important, and didna want to trust it to a telegram, or another," he explained. "No hard feelin's," he told Alex.

"Of course not," Alex replied. What else could he say?

"And I thought this one might need some assistance depending on who he encountered along the way. Ye ken?"

Brodie nodded.

"And the package?" I inquired.

Munro smiled, and I was reminded of the reasons Templeton had found him to be a most intriguing man.

His features were leaner than Brodie's but no less compelling with high cheek bones and that piercing blue gaze —very much like some Norse invader come to ravage and pillage.

"The package was sent by her ladyship."

I exchanged a look with Brodie as I went to the table and unwrapped the 'package' that was in fact a bottle of whisky.

"I hope ye did not reveal anything about our inquiry case," Brodie commented.

"Not the particulars," he assured us both. "However, I have learned there is little that her ladyship does not know about what goes on regarding her household, her family, and London for that matter. She does have her sources that would put the Agency to shame."

The last part was for Alex Sinclair's benefit.

"Yes, well, shall we get on with it?"

'It' was the information Sir Avery had indicated in that telegram Brodie received before we left Paris. A turn of events with the potential for devastating consequences to the Crown, and across the Empire.

I caught the look Alex gave Brodie, and that subtle change of expression on Brodie's face.

"What ye have to say, can be said to us all."

Ales nodded, then made his apologies to me. "It is only that this appears to be far more devastating than a mere gentlemen's weekend in the country."

"Go on," Brodie told him.

"There have been certain facts that have been uncovered by Sir Avery in his own efforts in this matter." Alex looked around the table, then continued in a low voice.

"It seems that Sir Collingwood was involved in the development of a certain type of machine."

"What sort of machine?" Brodie inquired.

"I only caught a glimpse of the drawing that Sir Avery acquired. It's some sort of aircraft."

"Aircraft?" I remarked. "What sort of aircraft? A balloon perhaps?"

"Something quite different. According to Sir Avery, they're calling it an air ship. It is propelled by a motor."

I thought of my adventure aloft in a previous case in a hot air a balloon. It did seem that technology might have moved forward.

"There's a bit more to it," Alex continued. "Since it is powered by a motor, it is not reliant on the wind to navigate and can be guided over the water, land, and mountains."

"What else?" Brodie inquired.

"It would be guided by a pilot and could carry certain cargo."

"What sort of cargo?"

"According to the drawing I saw, it could carry a bomb."

A bomb?

I looked over at Brodie. For what purpose?"

"There's more," Alex continued, after taking a sip of whisky.

"Sir Collingwood had the plans in his possession when he left for Sandringham for that weekend get-together, with the excuse that he was going to show them to His Highness."

Well and good, as far as it went. But there was obviously more.

"It seems that His Highness never saw the plans, nor was there any conversation regarding them."

Brodie was thoughtful.

My thoughts raced.

"And what would the purpose of such a thing be?"

"Perhaps to put down some aggression. And it would seem that Sir Collingwood might have chosen to share that information with someone else."

Someone he was to meet that last night at Sandringham, or perhaps afterwards taking advantage of his time away from London? But whom?

I thought of what Brodie and I had learned in our search of his private room at Sandringham, the footprints in the gardens that led to that horrible discovery, and then the information we'd managed to retrieve from his London residence.

I didn't mention any of that at the moment. Alex undoubtedly knew from Sir Avery what we'd learned before leaving London.

"There's more," Munro commented. "I encountered an acquaintance of yers, Herr Schmidt at the German Gymnasium."

I could imagine how that might have happened. It did appear that Brodie had shared that much with Munro.

"What was he able to learn?" Brodie aside.

"The man Szábo is Hungarian by birth. But over the past ten years he has established his 'business' in Frankfurt, Germany."

Ticklish situation indeed if it was true, given the royal family's connection to Germany through the Queen's marriage to Prince Albert years before.

Though my great-aunt was quite a young woman at the time, she remembered the wide-spread disapproval of the marriage.

Yet, over the years Prince Albert had proven the naysayers wrong with his loyalty to the English crown and the Queen, his efforts to improve conditions among the poor, and he had been the driving supporter of the Great Exhibition.

Their firstborn, also named Victoria, had then married Frederick III, the German Emperor, when she came of age, as the Queen had encouraged—some said manipulated—all her children to make royal attachments throughout Europe, including Russia, spreading the influence and power of the British Empire according to some.

It seemed unlikely that a man of Sir Collingwood's authority and reputation would be engaged in some nefarious undertakings. And yet...

"What sort of business activities?" I asked.

"Szábo provides information and opportunity to others, for a price," Munro replied.

Perhaps connections to potential buyers and sellers?

"Who are his customers?"

"As with any businessman, it would be the highest bidder," Brodie explained. "And for the greatest profit."

"Surely someone knows where he might be and what he might know."

"Herr Schmidt gave me the name of a man in Frankfurt," Munro then added.

"He is said to be an associate of Szábo, who goes by the name of Sebastian Bruhl. Although, according to Schmidt, no one has ever seen Bruhl and lived to speak of it."

"Did Herr Schmidt mention anything about a woman by the name of Angeline Cotillard?"

Munro shook his head. "There was no mention of that name."

Brodie turned to me. "What time does the new exhibit open at the museum?"

"At noon tomorrow," I replied from the information we had learned from that handbill found in Dornay's atelier.

"The man at the address we found at Sir Collingwood's residence had a handbill and travel papers for the opening of a new art exhibition at the Royal Museum beginning tomorrow," he explained. "He obviously planned to attend."

Sir Avery had made arrangements for Alex to have accommodations at the hotel as well. And that now included Munro who had chosen to accompany him.

Munro rose from his chair. "Then ye plan to go to the museum?"

"We might be able to learn something about the reason Dornay was to attend."

"Someone he was to meet there?"

Brodie nodded.

"That could be most difficult."

"Aye, however, the man was killed for a reason. And now, with the information provided by Herr Schmidt, it's not a thing to ignore."

"Then perhaps two more of us will be able to find somethin'." Munro looked over at Alex.

"Do you snore?"

"I don't know. Lucy has never mentioned..." Alex caught himself before revealing something more personal.

Lucy was the young woman he lived with. She had once worked for the Times of London newspaper, and I had first made her acquaintance in another inquiry case.

"What about a weapon? Did ye bring one?" Brodie asked.

"No, Sir Avery thought it best that I didn't. International borders, police and all that."

Munro nodded as he went to the door. "I always carry a blade."

He checked the hallway, then continued to the stairs that led to the third floor. Alex looked from Brodie to me.

"A blade?"

"Ye best not rouse him of a sudden during the night," Brodie warned. "Otherwise ye should be safe enough."

Alex laughed, a bit nervously I thought. As if he thought Brodie was making a joke at his expense.

"Of course."

"And best to check the hallway whenever ye come and go, as we dinna know who we're dealing with and it now seems as if the situation is more than murder," Brodie warned. "Best to remember that we are a long way from London and the Agency."

Alex nodded and bid us good night. It was amusing to watch him as he checked the hall outside our door, then nodded and continued after Munro.

"The information they brought could be helpful," I commented after he left.

"Perhaps. We will see what might be found at the art exhibit tomorrow."

A connection? Something that might reveal the reason Dornay was to attend? Or was it merely as an artist?

Perhaps. It was a word I heard often as he kept other thoughts to himself. I was quite used to it.

I went to the writing desk where I had taken out my notebook when we returned from supper.

"Have ye been to Frankfurt in yer travels?"

"I spent two days there on the return from Istanbul." So that was where his thoughts were.

"Aye." He poured us both a dram of whisky from the bottle Munro had brought, the last of it after the past hours.

"Historically it is the city of Charlemagne." Not that I expected him to know that.

"Ye donna say."

I smiled. "Eighth century, head of the religious council that condemned Adoptionism."

That dark gaze narrowed on me. "He was quite famous or infamous as it were and led the condemnation of Adoptionism which was the concept that Jesus had been adopted by God. The Catholic Church was very much against the idea."

"Ye are not Catholic."

I ignored the comment.

"The printing press was invented there by a man named Johannes Gutenberg. It completely revolutionized the printing of newspapers and books, for which I am extremely grateful."

He took a long sip of whisky as I sat at the desk to make my notes.

"Frankfurt has long been the center of German politics," I continued. "Over the past several years there have been conflicts between different groups, not unlike demonstrations by workers in other cities. And then there are those who feel that Frankfurt should never have been annexed by Prussia—long-standing conflict that goes back decades."

I looked up and found him watching me.

"What are you staring at, Mister Brodie?"

"Most ladies fill their days with trips to the dressmaker, late afternoon tea taken with other ladies, and evenings at the theater," he drily commented. "However, ye are fascinated by history, new inventions, and politics."

"Someone we both know told me a long time ago that I had a brain and it would be a shame not to use it."

There was that smile that often led to other things.

"Her ladyship, no doubt."

"I did not want to disappoint her."

"Ye are a rare one, Mikaela Forsythe."

Rare. I would take it.

I set aside my pen and crossed the small sitting room where he sat in an overstuffed chair, legs stretched before the fire. That empty glass dangled loose in his fingers.

Rare.

I bent and kissed him.

"It is quite late, Mr. Brodie..."

Fourteen

WE ROSE EARLY in the morning with several hours before the opening of the new art exhibit at the museum.

We ate, then I returned to our room to go over the notes that I had made the day before.

I sat tapping my pen on the writing desk as Brodie returned from meeting with Munro and Alex to set the plan for attending the exhibit at the Royal Museum.

When in London, I was used to various sources of information that included both known persons, acquaintances of my great-aunt—she did have a great deal of influence—and the archives of the dailies that had proven to be a source of helpful information in the past.

However, here in Brussels, I felt like a fish out of water, cut off from my usual resources and in a situation that had become far more than just murder.

There were now two murders to be precise, along with the information Alex and Munro had brought from London—that Sir Collingwood might very well have been involved in passing information regarding new military developments on to foreign characters.

But there were far too many unknowns. For what reason would he pass highly secret information onto to those foreign characters? What part did Angeline Cotillard play in this? Lover? Foreign agent, as Alex Sinclair had called her?

What of a man named Szábo, and Sebastian Bruhl? They lived in the shadows, Szábo associated in the past with anarchist groups. As for Bruhl? Virtually nothing was known beyond the information that Sir Avery had provided.

There had to be more. As Brodie had once said, even rats who lived in the shadows emerged from time to time. It was just a matter of knowing when, and then trapping the rat when it came out of those shadows.

Easier said than done, I thought.

"Wot are ye thinkin' now?"

"It could be helpful to see if there is other information about either Szábo or Bruhl that might be useful," I pointed out before he could point out that Sir Avery had access to more information than anyone else, perhaps in all of Britain.

"Lucy Penworth has been an incredible help in the past." I reminded him of Alex's fiancée. "She is intelligent and resourceful, and quite daring."

"She is also employed by the Agency."

I knew his meaning.

"This would be information the Agency might not think important—a rumor, reported sightings, gossip about a mistress perhaps...that might be accessed elsewhere."

"Angeline Cotillard?" he commented.

"It is possible. Templeton did suggest that she was known to have several affairs. And she was at Sandringham that weekend. Such things might not be found to be important at the time and mere filler for newspaper stories. However..." I paused.

"And there has been no sighting or information about Angeline since, that we know of. It could be important to find out where she is and perhaps what she knows."

"How do you propose to send Miss Penworth a message? If Avery were to discover it, it could go bad for her."

I had thought about that. "There is someone who has access to the Agency, who is above reproach, could be persuaded to take a message to Lucy. And, she is someone you trust as well, as I recall." I let that sink in.

"Good God, Mikaela! You cannot mean...! She is eighty-five years old, and not up to this sort of thing."

"Eighty-six years old her last birthday," I corrected him. "And she has grown quite bored since our return from Africa."

I was able to learn the nearest location of a telegraph office from the front desk manager.

We had made arrangements to meet Munro and Alex at the main entrance to the Royal Museum for the grand opening of the new fine art exhibit. We then went to the telegraph office to send off the telegram to my great-aunt.

Brodie accompanied me to a nearby counter in the telegraph office where I composed my message to Lady Antonia Montgomery. It was quite simple and yet there was a message behind the words I knew she would understand:

Please give Lucy my kindest regards.
She has been most helpful in the planning for the event.
Need her advice regarding the two gentlemen.
Send reply as soon as possible c/o the Hotel Castelon, Brussels.
With our regards. M.

"Ye believe that Lucy will understand yer meaning?"

"As I said, she's very clever and resourceful. Alex would do well to marry her."

"And her ladyship?"

"She will be thrilled to assist us. You know, she is quite fond of you."

I paid the attendant at the telegraph office extra to send the message off immediately.

"Planning a wedding is most exciting," I told him in French as an added element, to not stir undue curiosity.

"*Oui*, madame."

"I will have to remember that ye are given to a stretch of the truth from time to time," Brodie commented as we found a driver.

The Museum of Fine Arts had originally opened in the former palace of Charles of Lorraine, according to the slightly blood-stained handbill we had discovered in that apartment in Paris.

It had gone through several locations until 1881, when the first rooms of the new location were opened. It had since expanded, along with the other museums that dominated the site—five in total, with another soon planned, according to additional information we received as we were joined by Munro and Alex, and entered the museum.

"This is most impressive," Alex commented as we joined the queue with other patrons who had come to view the works of living artists.

"What are we lookin' for?" Munro asked.

It was actually a very good question. I had no idea, although we had explained how we had learned about the exhibition that had seemed important to Monsieur Dornay.

"Perhaps a conversation that is overheard," Brodie suggested. "With the names we spoke of and accents that ye dinna recognize. It might be useful to move apart. The event seemed to have importance for the man we found."

"A conversation, those two names, and an accent in a room full of accents," Munro commented. "Is there anythin' else?"

"I didn't realize that sarcasm was a Scottish trait," I commented in lowered voice as he and Alex both moved away from us as if casually inspecting the artwork on display.

"He's used to more obvious clues," Brodie replied.

"Stolen goods? The obvious criminal sort, with a mask, hat pulled low? Perhaps some blood?" I suggested.

"Let us say that art is not how he would choose to spend an afternoon."

"Nor yourself for that matter?"

"I leave the art to ye and yer sister," Brodie commented as he stepped across the aisle, while I continued in the line of patrons as we slowly moved through the hall, observing the works of living artists.

Living artists? The thought came back.

Was it possible that Monsieur Dornay's plans to travel to Brussels were in fact because he was to have one of his works on display?

I looked for Brodie as the thought persisted. While I was no expert in the works of artists, I did recognize genuine talent. And in spite of the circumstances in that apartment, it was obvious that Monsieur Dornay was quite talented.

We had received a list of artists whose works were on display as we arrived. I quickly scanned the list and found his name.

According to the brochure, he had two paintings on

display. One was called '*Fin De Journée,*' translated from French for 'End of Day,' the second one was simply '*La Fille,*' 'The Girl.'

I looked again for Brodie but he had disappeared into the crowd. I then looked for either Alex or Munro, but had no success there. Unable to find any one of them, I continued through the crowd with a new urgency, quickly scanning the placards in front of each artist's works, then moving to the next.

I found the display I was looking for and stared at them. Both were in a similar style as Monet.

The first one, *La Fille,* was a portrait of a young girl standing in a garden with a bouquet in her hand. The second painting, *Fin de Journée,* was of a young woman with golden blonde hair drawn back from her face as she turned, dark eyes staring back over her shoulder at the artist, with a tentative smile on vivid red lips.

I glanced back at the first one, studying it. Then at the second one once more. The subject was the same, only painted perhaps a few years apart! As a young girl with a look of innocence upon her face, and then the somewhat older young woman. The expression on her face and in her eyes told a different story. The innocent young girl no longer existed.

In addition to the fact that the two were obviously the same person, what was I looking at?

Artistic talent to be certain, a beautiful young model...I then realized what it was.

The young woman in both paintings was identical to the model in that painting at Dornay's studio! In both paintings, at the studio and the young woman I now looked at, the subject wore bright red lipstick! A shade I had seen before, on that cigar and in Collingwood's bedchamber, at Sandringham.

Was it possible they were one and the same?

"Miss Forsythe!"

There was only one person among my companions who still called me that, force of habit I suspect. I turned as Alex Sinclair came toward me through the crowd of people.

Two things then happened almost at the same time. A figure darted toward me. He was short, no taller than a child, a knife clutched in one hand.

He was extremely quick. As instinct took over, I sidestepped, thrust my foot under, sent him sprawling to the floor, and pulled the knife from my boot.

Quick as a cat, he rolled, sprang back to his feet and lunged at me.

"I've got him, Miss Forsythe," Alex called out as he charged to my defense.

The little man grinned as he spun away from me, somersaulted, then slashed at Alex as he rolled back to his feet, tossed a look back at me, then disappeared through the crowd of stunned, screaming bystanders who were only just becoming aware of the assault among them.

I ran to Alex. He looked up at me with a startled expression.

"Are you all right, Miss Forsythe?"

"Yes, of course..." I assured him, then saw the blood on the front of his shirt.

"I tried to stop him..." He was quite pale and unsteady on his feet. "Oh, my..."

He swayed toward me and would have gone down if Brodie hadn't reached us. He caught him about the shoulders, then looked at me

"Ye have blood all over ye."

I heard that sound low in his voice that I had heard before
—calm but with that edge.

"It's not mine. I'm all right."

"Are ye certain?"

"Yes, I'm afraid it's poor Alex who's been badly wounded."

He nodded then. "We need to get him away from here," he said in that same low voice as those around us stared while others simply moved on as if it was an everyday occurrence to attend an art exhibit in the museum and have a man slashed in their midst.

Munro had joined us by now, and quickly assessed the situation.

"I'm all right," I assured him as that cold blue gaze swept over me.

"Did ye see who did this?"

"A small man, no taller than my waist, dressed in everyday work clothes, boots," and something that came back as shock gave way to anger.

"He had a tattoo on the side of his neck."

Munro nodded and he was off, pushing his way through the crowd as Brodie supported Alex, barely conscious, and I led the way from the exhibit hall.

Munro joined us outside the museum.

"I lost him in the crowd. How bad is he wounded?"

"Bad enough," Brodie replied as Munro waived down a driver, that well-known gesture that needed no translation.

We were fortunate that most of the people were still arriving for the exhibit, as Munro held open the door of a coach as the passengers disembarked, then assisted Brodie getting Alex inside.

They climbed in after, then Brodie held out a hand to me. I climbed in as Munro gave the driver the name of our hotel.

Alex sat propped up against Munro as I lifted my skirt and tore a length of muslin from my slip then folded it.

"Open his shirt," I told Munro. I then pressed the folded muslin low on his stomach where our attacker had slashed him.

"Ye've a steady hand for such things," Munro commented. "For a lady."

I exchanged a look with Brodie as our coach lurched through late afternoon traffic toward our hotel. That dark gaze held mine.

"I had a good teacher." I reminded him of the lessons he had given me before I set off on my first adventure. "And I've had a bit of practice," I added as I recalled a cut or two that I'd bandaged for Brodie. However, nothing like this.

I took a deep breath and steadied my fingers as I tied the loose ends of his shirt across the thick bandage.

It seemed to take forever to reach our hotel. But in truth we returned rather quickly.

Brodie paid the driver as Munro assisted Alex from the coach. I smoothed my bloodied skirt and followed. Brodie closed the front of his jacket over his equally bloodied shirt.

"A bit too much of the drink," Munro explained to the startled desk manager as they assisted Alex to the stairs. The manager merely nodded and smiled.

Out of sight of the front desk, Munro hoisted Alex over his shoulder much like a sack of grain, and continued up the stairs to the room they shared on the third floor. Brodie and I followed.

Munro deposited Alex on the bed in the adjacent chamber as I set aside my travel bag and then removed my hat and jacket.

"I will need the rest of that whisky from our room," I said as I sat at the bed beside Alex. He was conscious although still very pale.

I untied the tail ends of his shirt and carefully lifted that impromptu bandage.

"I will need towels," I told Munro. "And my shift from our room," I told Brodie.

"Your shift?" Alex replied incredulously as he craned his neck to see the extent of the damage his knife-wielding attacker had caused as I removed makeshift bandage that had once been a portion of my slip.

His head fell back to the bed, the effort exhausting him after the loss of blood.

"Is she always like this?" he whispered.

"Aye," Brodie replied with a look at me as he headed for our room. "Best get used to it."

When he returned, I used a small towel from the bathroom to clean the blood from slash marks as best could be done.

"I will need his razor," I told Munro. While Alex wore a neatly trimmed mustache, it was obvious he used a razor for the rest of his grooming.

His pale expression turned a bit green.

"What do you need my razor for?"

Munro had retrieved it from the bathroom and I proceeded to cut the chemise that Brodie had brought from our room into manageable strips for a new bandage.

"I've never worn a lady's shift," Alex quipped, remarkable under the circumstances.

"It looks quite charming on you," I teased him right back as I doused one of the towels with the last of the whisky, then gently applied the towel to the three slash wounds.

Alex gasped and sucked in a deep breath of air. "Bloody hell! Beg your pardon, Miss Mikaela. Dear God, that hurts..."

"It's quite all right," I assured him. "I've heard far worse."

"And she's said far worse," Brodie commented.

Alex looked up at me. "Am I going to die? If so, I do need to write a note for Lucy."

How touching, I thought.

"I've seen worse, aye," Munro looked over at Brodie who nodded in agreement.

"Ye'll live fer certain. No need to write a note. But ye will need a physician."

I agreed. "I do wish Mr. Brimley was here. He would be able to apply one of his antiseptic tonics, perhaps even apply stitches to close one of these."

"Stitches?" Alex exclaimed. "With a needle?"

"Nothin' to it, lad. Just a wee prick of the skin," Munro explained. "Pullin' the thread through is the worst of it."

Alex paled even further now with a green tinge about the mouth. So much for the brave young man who had chased down a bomber in a previous case.

I was in agreement. Two of the marks had ceased bleeding and in Mr. Brimley's educated opinion in past situations would undoubtedly heal on their own with medicinal salve that I was familiar with. The third cut, however, was deeper through the skin to the tissue below and continued to seep blood.

"It could be risky to seek out a physician here," Brodie said with a nod from Munro.

"Too many questions that might bring on the local authorities."

I understood. Two people were dead, Alex had been attacked by that little man, whom I now realized I had glimpsed before at the rail station. A coincidence? I was now doubtful.

And there was the matter of the man called Szábo and another named Bruhl who were somehow connected to the murder of Sir Collingwood.

The last thing we needed was for the German authorities to become involved. It was more important than ever that we be able to continue our investigation of the case.

Brodie and Munro often communicated with a look or a few words, from their time since boyhood. I caught the look Brodie gave him now.

"Aye," Munro agreed. "I will see him back to London."

"The sooner the better," I told him. "Before infection sets in."

"There's no need," Alex weakly protested.

"You've done what you can here by bringing us word from Sir Avery. You must now look to your own injury. You can trust Munro."

He nodded then closed his eyes as he laid back on the bed.

The plan was set. Munro was to see Alex to the same rail station they had arrived at. From there they would travel on to Calais, and then Dover, retracing the route we had taken. It was a trip of a full day and more, depending on the connections they were able to make.

Yet there was the possibility that Munro would be able to get word to Sir Avery once they reached Paris. With the connections Sir Avery seemed to have on the Continent, Alex might be able to get medical attention there before continuing on to London.

Brodie made inquiries about the rail schedule through the front desk manager. A train was leaving early the next morning from the Brussels rail station, arriving in Paris just before noon. Munro would be able to contact London from a telegraph dispatch office there.

We would accompany them to the Brussels station and send a message off to London with the information about their arrival in Paris, and an update that we were continuing on with the case.

Munro would be able to provide additional information regarding the recent developments when he and Alex were safely back in London.

With a little help from my great-aunt's whisky, Alex spent a quiet night. Munro changed his bandages when needed, while Brodie and I returned to our own room.

"I recognized the man who attacked Alex," I told him as I sat at the writing desk and made the new notes about the day's events. "I'm certain of it now. He was at the rail station in Paris. And he fits the description Templeton gave me of the man who travels with Angeline Cotillard."

Brodie nodded. "With what has happened, it would seem that the man followed us here and is responsible for the attack that was meant for ye."

I had thought about that as well. It was obvious that I was the intended target, and then Alex had intervened. I waited for all the reasons that I should return to London with them.

Somewhat to my surprise there were none. Instead, Brodie opened his valise and took out that revolver that was usually in the drawer of the desk in the office. He handed it to me.

"If ye wore trousers I would tell ye to put it in yer pocket. Since ye dinna wear them, put it in yer bag. It's loaded. If ye have another such encounter, yer to use it to protect yerself."

"The authorities here or in Frankfurt might object to that," I pointed out.

He nodded. "Then they can deal with me. I won't have ye in danger if it can be avoided."

I took the revolver and tucked it into my bag. I was quite proficient with it after lessons he and Munro had both provided, and the fact that I had been around hunting weapons as a young child. I had a healthy respect for them, a weapon of last resort that I had been forced to use in the past.

"You're not going to tell me that I'm not to continue with you to Frankfurt?"

There was that look, that dark gaze meeting mine.

"Would it do any good to tell ye what I want is for you to go back tomorrow with the two of them?"

Rather than a blunt answer he already knew, I decided on a different tactic.

"You don't speak German," I pointed out.

While my own familiarity with the language was limited to the usual sort a tourist would speak, still I knew several places including the rail station along with the hotel where I'd once stayed, and I was convinced I could be of help.

Frankfurt was a modern city that included international banking as I had discovered on my travels through there. As with Paris and Brussels, it was very possible that English was spoken as well.

Brodie retrieved supper for us from the dining room, along with a couple bottles of wine, all which we shared with Munro. Alex had no appetite. Munro gave him the last of the whisky and he dozed fitfully, waking groggy from loss of blood and no food, then dozing once more.

Brodie explained to Munro that I had seen the attacker before in Paris, and according to that information from Templeton, the man was known to travel with Angeline Cotillard.

"Best take necessary measures in case the man followed us from the museum today. He won't want to be caught.

"I would like very much for him to come here," Munro replied and took out the knife he always carried. He ran his thumb along the sharp edge, his meaning quite clear.

I sat at the desk after we returned to our own room, and made a few additional entries into my notebook. A fire burned in the fireplace, but I couldn't seem to get warm.

It would have been a lie to say that the day's events hadn't affected me. While I constantly shifted about to get comfortable or startled at a sound at the hallway outside our door, Brodie was calm if a bit distracted as he sat in that overstuffed chair before the fire and smoked his pipe.

He eventually moved about, checking that the lock was set on the door, then took off his suit coat and laid it over the back of the chair.

I made the last of my notes, then sat back at the desk.

Since working with Brodie, I had learned a great deal about the criminal mind. Those three words came to mind.

Motive, means, and opportunity.

According to the information Alex and Munro had brought from London, the motive seemed to be providing military secrets to someone willing to purchase them.

In this particular instance, that would be someone who had used Angeline Cotillard, and took advantage of her close relationship with the Prince of Wales and his inner circle. Most particularly Sir Collingwood.

There was the question if she was not only his Royal Highness's mistress, but also Collingwood's.

Sir Collingwood most certainly had the means in his work as Lord of the Admiralty, and the opportunity. Never mind that the opportunity had gotten him killed.

I did suppose that was one way to avoid the hangman's rope.

I felt Brodie's hands on my shoulders.

"Come away, lass. There's nothin' more that can be done tonight, but plenty enough in the mornin'."

I tucked my pen inside my notebook and then slipped both inside my travel bag.

Preparing for bed was somewhat simpler than before. I stepped out of my skirt and shirtwaist, then my long slip which was now missing several inches around the hem.

My night shift had been used for bandages along as well.

"Dinna bother." He removed his trousers and shirt. "I'll buy ye a new one. And no one will ever know that yer not wearin' one."

I shivered as I removed the pins from my hair. We had not built a fire. I shook my hair loose then slipped under the blankets on the bed. Then Brodie was there.

"Ye did well today, lass." His arm went around me and he pulled me back against him. "Alex may well owe ye his life."

"The bleeding has stopped. Now the worry is infection. But he should be all right when Munro gets him back to London." I waited as we lay together.

Alex had made no secret of the fact that the attack at the museum was obviously meant for me.

I braced myself for the usual objections, that it was too dangerous, and that he wanted me to return to London as well, even though we had already discussed it.

"Aren't you going to tell me that it would be best for me to return to London?" I waited again.

Then, "No."

That one small word, with enormous meaning. I turned so that we were facing one another.

I traced that scar that sliced through his left brow, so very close to the eye, an encounter in our last case. He wasn't the only one who worried over someone, the risks *he* took, other injuries that eventually healed.

"It would do no good. I know that. And I trust that ye are

strong, and wise, although ye do have a bit of temper from time to time.

He picked up a thick strand of my hair from my shoulders.

"Are ye certain there isn't a fierce Viking among yer ancestors with all that fine red hair?"

I shivered slightly, though not from the cold. He did have that effect on me.

"Very possible," I replied, then curled against him.

Fifteen

ALEX WAS NO BETTER in the morning, but also no worse. Except for the fever. That had me worried. According to Mr. Brimley it was a sign of infection and even more critical that Munro at least get him back to Paris as soon as possible.

Failing that and any assistance Sir Avery might be able to provide with those he knew, Munro was to take him back to London straight away and to Mr. Brimley.

"Dinna worry, miss," Munro assured me as I again placed a hand on Alex's forehead.

"I'll see that he gets back safely."

"I'm certain you will." If not Brodie, there was no one else I would have trusted more.

We said our farewells at the rail station, even as it was not lost on me that Brodie kept a continual eye on our surroundings, those who arrived and those who departed.

"Ye have a weapon?" he asked Munro.

There was that smile, slow, and yet not precisely a smile. It was more what I might have expected of Rupert the hound when he came upon someone he didn't like. Except for the teeth.

"Always, as ye know."

Brodie nodded as the call went out for their departure. There was no shaking of the hand, no last-minute word of advice. They merely nodded to each other as I had seen dozens of times—silent messages passed along that each understood.

I laid a hand on Alex's arm, and thanked him for attempting to aid me the day before, at the cost to himself

"Not at all, Miss Forsythe," he replied with a game smile.

Farewells were said and Brodie helped Munro get him aboard their compartment. I did think that they looked a bit like three friends who had stayed at the local tavern until the wee hours of the morning as they supported Alex between them.

"He will be all right, lass," Brodie said when he returned, his watchful look surveying others at the station who waited to board or see others on their way.

"He could not be in better hands than Munro."

I nodded. "I know. It's just that..."

"It wasna yer fault. There was no way to know wot would happen, and Alex did what came natural, which was to protect ye."

"I could have handled that wee bugger," I replied as anger took the place of other emotions.

"Aye, and perhaps in that, the 'wee bugger' was fortunate...this time. Next time, perhaps."

I could have sworn there was a smile there. I looked over at him. "*When,* not *if,* there is a next time, I will see the matter done to the wretched creature."

"Ah, no longer a wee bugger?"

He was teasing, and I supposed that was the only way to

look at the situation. For now. But there would be payback. I silently promised myself.

"Ye perhaps understand wot it is to see someone ye care about injured or worse."

I did understand. However…

"Come along, now," he said then, as the train began to move, slowly at first as it pulled from the station, then gathering more speed as it left the rail yard.

"We need to see if there is any word from Miss Lucy."

There were two telegrams waiting for us. One from Lucy, the second from my great-aunt. Brodie opened Aunt Antonia's telegram first. He read it to himself, a slight frown forming.

"For heaven's sake. What does she have to say?" I asked.

I expected what would have been the usual, informing us that Lucy would be in contact, a reminder to be careful. That foreigners could not be trusted. Perhaps an update on the wedding plans, and then the usual question about when we might be returning regarding said wedding plans.

However, this was my great-aunt, someone I loved dearly, who had lived her life so far quite outside the usual constraints of society. Someone, I had learned quite young, who was predictably unpredictable.

At Brodie's prolonged silence, I became quite anxious. Had she taken a fall? Had she been out and about in her motor carriage again and suffered an accident? Or was it about Lily? Some mishap? Had she run away, as she had recently threatened over her lessons? Something I could sympathize with, though I would never say it.

"Oh, for heaven's sake." I grabbed the telegram from him.

"Greetings, my dears. *'L'* will be replying directly with *info.*"

Info?

Good heavens, an abbreviation and referring to Lucy as *"L,"* no doubt my great-aunt's version of using code words.

If the situation wasn't so dire, I would have laughed as I continued to read.

"Sir Laughton was most helpful and have added Herr Johannes Wagner, Kaiserstrasse, Frankfurt, to the guest list. Have wired intro if you should call on him. Regards.

She had not added her name. I did notice that the telegram had been sent under another name.

"Sir Laughton, her attorney," I commented as I folded the telegram and put it in my travel bag. And a contact we now had in Frankfurt through him.

"What does Lucy have to say about the inquiries she was to make?"

"The Times, one year ago; person you mentioned-S; substantial criminal record; charged with murder, escaped, last seen in Frankfurt, Germany, June this year; known associate S. Bruhl leader of criminal group responsible for kidnapping, robbery, smuggling, extortion. Said to keep company with an actress from the theater."

"Bruhl appears to be a well-rounded fellow," I sarcastically commented. I could only assume that the 'actress' Lucy mentioned, might be Angeline Cotillard.

"And verra dangerous with those activities," Brodie replied.

"I should respond to Lucy's telegram," I said then. "She deserves to know about Alex, and reassure her that he will be all right."

"It is best we don't communicate more than absolutely

necessary," Brodie replied. "If we're to have a chance of finding Szábo."

I knew that he was right. We had considerably more than when we set out that morning. We now had information on both Szábo and Bruhl, as well as someone who might be able to provide additional information.

I shook my head. There was another worry.

"Wot is it?"

"Except for that first case that involved Linnie, I have always tried to keep my family out of what we do."

"Her ladyship?"

I nodded. "She is, after all, eighty-six years old."

He looked at me and I could have sworn there was amusement in that dark gaze.

"And ye thought to protect her."

"It was a simple request to contact Lucy Penworth, nothing more, and now she's involved in this...What are you looking at?"

"Lady Antonia Montgomery," he replied. "And ye forget I have had some experience working with her in the past. She does exactly as she pleases..."

I understood his meaning quite well.

"Ye are exactly alike."

It was just like him to get the last word in.

We returned to our hotel. I had the clothes I had worn the day before out to be cleaned, and had hand-washed my shirtwaist and what was left of my slip, then hung them to dry on hooks.

Having traveled in some uncertain areas on my adventures had prepared me to take care of many things myself. I had also hand-laundered Brodie's shirt from the day before.

As yesterday, Brodie had placed a piece of paper in at the door against any unwanted visitors. It was still there when we returned.

Whoever that little man was who had attacked Alex, it did not seem that he had followed us back to our hotel.

With the information I had from Templeton, that Angeline traveled in the company of a small man, it seemed possible that, whoever he was, he might very well have taken himself off to Frankfurt.

What was he to her? Bodyguard? Lover? Fellow thief? And now murderer?

It was possible, given the weapon he had used against Alex, that he might very well have murdered Sir Collingwood. But for what reason?

As part of the scheme to obtain those highly secret drawings of the air ship as Sir Avery had learned? And then eliminate anyone along the way who might be able to identify them?

"I know that frown," Brodie commented as he returned from a walk about the street where the hotel was located, and a conversation with the manager for a substantial amount of compensation. He had been gone an extremely long time.

However, that gave me the opportunity to make the latest notes, and I had then destroyed both telegrams, the paper smoldering in the ash dish on the table before the hearth in the sitting room. No need to leave them lying about for someone else to read.

I went back over everything we'd learned, including that information that Alex had brought with him, along with the information Munro had learned from Schmidt. His brother-in-law worked in one of the outer districts of Frankfurt. It was a city he knew well. There had also been the name of an inn.

Cober Haus Inn, very near Kaiserstrasse in the main part of the city.

"Based on the information Munro brought from Herr Schmidt, it would seem that his brother-in-law might be quite motivated to assist us."

"Aye."

"And with the name we now have from Sir Laughton, we have someone else we can contact." I thought of the attorney in Frankfurt

"Perhaps."

I heard the hesitation in his voice. "You are doubtful."

"We will see. We will call on the man. It could be useful. While he may be an associate by profession, it would be good to remember that he may very well have interests of his own that lie elsewhere. We are foreigners, asking his assistance. We need to be careful."

I had learned that, even in the East End of London, it was often those in positions less fortunate who could be trusted over others.

There was a train departing Brussels for Frankfurt at eight o'clock in the morning.

My skirt and jacket along with a pair of Brodie's trousers had been returned late that afternoon.

I had done the best I could with his jacket and the substantial amount of dried blood from Alex's encounter with his attacker. Our shirts had to be hand-washed. I thought it best that the laundress not see all that blood. So I proceeded to soak them in the basin in the bathroom.

Brodie watched with an expression that was a cross between doubt and amazement.

"I still canna believe that ye know how to wash yer own clothes!"

"And yours as well, Mr. Brodie," I replied. "Water, soap, a good scrubbing. Swirl things about in a basin, apply soap, bath soap in this case, scrub well, then rinse, wring out the water, and hang to dry." I demonstrated.

"A lady who does her own laundry. I'm verra impressed."

That comment along with the expression on his face was taking things a bit far. I threw his wadded-up but still soggy shirt at him, hitting him square in the middle of that smug expression.

"What do you think our chances are finding those documents that went missing at Sandringham?" We had brought a meal to our room as our laundry dried before the hearth.

Dinner included a fare of beef and potatoes, with sliced fresh-baked bread, and a bottle of wine.

He frowned over his glass, then set it on the table.

"Considering the amount of time that's passed since Sir Collingwood was murdered, it is possible it has already been sold off to the highest bidder."

"Or not?" I suggested. It did seem possible that the documents had not been sold to anyone as yet, particularly after the encounter with the little man who was a known companion of Angeline Cotillard.

"If not," Brodie continued, "after that encounter at the museum, there will be every attempt to sell them. The only hope we have is the amount demanded.

"For those like Szábo and Bruhl, it is all about the highest price the documents can bring on the open market, 'foreign actors,' who would be interested in purchasing them."

Foreign actors—I thought that an interesting choice of words considering Angeline Cotillard's profession.

"That drives the cost up to the highest bidder," he continued. "It could be any one of a half-dozen possible buyers."

"Like an auction," I replied.

"Aye. Because of that, my guess would be that Bruhl does not yet have the documents. It is possible that Szábo either might have yet to make contact with Bruhl, or is holding onto them for his own purposes while putting out the word to others."

"He would double-cross Bruhl?"

"Cross, double-cross," Brodie replied.

That was interesting. No doubt something he'd learned living on the streets as a boy.

"I thought there was honor among thieves."

"Only so far, lass. Then it is every man, or woman, for themselves."

"Angeline Cotillard?" Was it possible that she still had the documents?

"It would depend on whose bed she's sleeping in now."

Cross, double-cross.

We rose early in order to depart Brussels on that morning train. In spite of my clean skirt and jacket, I chose to wear my walking skirt, boots, and freshly washed shirtwaist.

I had a reason, of course, for wearing the walking skirt. Brodie would have thought it very amusing.

One must always be prepared.

To that end, I had secured the blade in my boot, and the revolver into the deep pocket I had the dressmaker include when she made the skirt, in the style of one my friend

Templeton had given me after the return from her American tour.

Most handy, as she described the style, which had become quite popular the past few years across London for women who participated in lawn sports, tennis, equestrian events, and shooting sports.

There was still a long way to go before they would be allowed to compete in official competitions, of course. I suspected personally that it had more to do with men being concerned over those sports with a mallet, or the shooting sports.

We boarded our train without incident, both of us watchful for any sign of that little man. However, there was none. It was possible that he had already left Brussels to join Angeline Cotillard?

We settled back in our compartment for the five-hour trip that would take us to Frankfurt and our search for those stolen secret documents.

Sixteen

FRANKFURT, GERMANY

WE ARRIVED in Frankfurt on schedule. The main rail station was a sprawling behemoth under curved roofs with panels of glass that provided light and arched over the main building. It covered a dozen tracks with trains that arrived from and departed to various cities across Europe and beyond.

Brodie kept a firm hand on my arm as we left our compartment and navigated our way to the carriage station according to overhead signage.

We had discovered on the trip from Brussels that, while the most common language in Frankfurt was German, most merchants, tradesmen, and professional persons in banking and other enterprises also spoke English.

Quite well, an attendant from Frankfurt assured a fellow passenger. We had navigated Brussels efficiently with my background in French lessons from when my sister and I attended private school in Paris.

Along the way in my various travels, I had made it a habit of learning the basics for whichever country I visited.

I had a passable knowledge of Italian along with Portuguese when visiting Lisbon.

However, I had never managed Greek. It had not seemed necessary at the time. There were other ways to communicate. And then there was Gaelic, which I was still learning, word by individual word. But again, there were some things that needed no words.

At the carriage station, we discovered what they called a hansom carriage, very similar to hansom cabs in London. Brodie hired the driver and gave him the address of Herr Wagner's office on Kaiserstrasse in the main part of the city.

As I had also learned on my travels, having the appropriate currency could be an issue. However, our driver had no problem taking our French currency.

In heavily accented English he explained that he accepted most primary currencies in addition to German. That included French and English. It was the nature of the business at the rail stations. Even in the city proper, he assured us. Still, there were banks in the business district that could provide us with German marks.

The ride from the rail station to the main business district took very near an hour in midday traffic, much like London.

It was very near three o'clock in the afternoon when he finally navigated traffic-filled streets and we arrived at the address for Herr Wagner, his name displayed on a plaque along with the names of several others at the front of the building.

The city was a mixture of newer four-story concrete brick buildings in the classical style with an occasional ornamental domed cupola at the top floor for decoration. Remnants of older medieval-style buildings stood here and there, having survived the city's expansion, so far.

That 'modernization,' as our driver lamented, included a

horse-drawn trolley system on tracks, rumored soon to be replaced with electric trolleys.

"Progress," Brodie drily commented as I stepped down from the hansom cab.

While I was in favor of progress that included water and sewage systems, and electric in London that had much improved the city by eliminating a good many of what were referred to as 'slum' areas, I did see his point.

"You are old-fashioned," I commented as we climbed the steps into the foyer of the building. "I would never have guessed."

There was no reply as we approached a wood-enclosed desk and platform that looked very much like a pulpit. A woman in a stark black gown with white collar and cuffs at the wrists greeted us. Brodie gave Herr Wagner's name.

There was no response as she stared at us. I sensed Brodie rapidly losing patience. It might have been the way his mouth thinned as he addressed her next.

"If you please, madame. He is expecting us. Or, shall I start with the first-floor offices?"

"Of course," she snapped.

It seemed that she both understood and spoke English quite well.

The building on Kaiserstrasse was one of the newer ones that included a telephone system much like I had seen in London, with a half-dozen call tubes.

She made a call with one of those tubes, relayed a message to the party on the other end in rapid-fire German.

"Your names?"

"Lady Forsythe and Mr. Brodie," he informed her, which did raise one rather bushy eyebrow on the woman.

She repeated our names, then closed the call. Within a

matter of moments there was a buzzing sound at her desk. She answered the call.

There was a brief exchange in German, then she put down the handset.

"An attendant will escort you to Herr Wagner's office. You will wait here."

We waited.

Within only a few moments, a young man appeared, fresh-faced with blonde hair, brown eyes, and a polite smile.

"If you will follow me, please."

We followed.

There was a lift at the end of the entry hall. We stepped inside the cage and the attendant closed the gate, then engaged the lift that rose to the second floor. He stepped out, bowed, then indicated that we were to follow him.

Herr Wagner greeted us as he stepped out of his private office. The young man bowed again, then promptly disappeared.

Greetings were exchanged.

He was a pleasant-looking man, about the same age as Sir Laughton, with a steady blue gaze that I suspected missed nothing, and a congenial but speculative smile.

"I have been expecting you. Safe travel from Brussels?"

Brodie assured him that we had.

"What is it that I may assist with? My good friend, Sir Laughton, said only that it was of utmost importance that I make myself available upon your arrival in a matter that is most urgent."

I complimented him on his almost perfect English with only a hint of an accent. The courteous expression turned to a bemused smile.

"Sir Laughton and I studied at university in London

together, and then we both apprenticed to Sir Henry Asquith. After a four-year apprenticeship where I obtained a broad experience in the English legal system, I returned to Frankfurt and apprenticed here for two more years before establishing my own practice.

"There is much to be said about the bond of friendship," he continued. "We have since shared cases, my friend in London, and myself here where I can be of help to him, at times when others will not.

"I cannot share the details of these things with you, but perhaps he will tell you as much as he can when you return." He looked from Brodie to me. "How may I help you?"

Brodie watched him as he began to explain the case beginning with Sir Collingwood's murder.

"There has been a serious situation. The Lord of the Admiralty, Sir Collingwood, has been killed and important documents are now missing. It is thought that they were stolen. We have some information in the matter that we are following. We need your assistance in this."

He then mentioned the names of the two men we know were involved—Szábo and Bruhl.

Herr Wagner sat back in his desk chair and studied both of us for several moments.

"I understand that you were a detective with the Metropolitan Police in London. You have undoubtedly encountered different criminal elements. It is no different here. There are the usual crimes found in any large city—assault, robbery, petty thievery among street vendors, young men making mischief, that sort of thing..."

We did not know how much Sir Laughton had revealed of the information my great-aunt had provided. She knew almost nothing about the case.

I did understand that it was important to be as discreet as possible about the reason we were there. On the ride from the rail station, Brodie and I had discussed just how much information we needed to provide Herr Wagner for such a delicate matter as the theft of highly secret information.

"It is a bit more than petty thievery, sir," Brodie now replied. "We are here on behalf of the Crown. And in view of the close relations between our countries, most particularly on behalf of Her Majesty the Queen, we have been sent to set aright a certain matter."

He paused and let that sink in. Nothing like firing a cannon across the bow of the ship, I thought. It would, of course, be quite easy for Herr Wagner to verify the reason we were there, which Brodie obviously intended that he would do.

*When in Germany...*I thought.

"It is in the matter of a theft and the murder of a high-ranking official," Brodie continued. "We have been given complete authority to act on behalf of the Crown. My partner, Lady Forsythe, is representative of Her Majesty in this matter."

That was a bit more of a stretch of the truth, however I could play my part. I nodded at the introduction.

As much as Brodie was inclined not to use either my title or my connection through my great-aunt, there were instances where it could be advantageous. I did wonder precisely how Herr Wagner would react.

"I see," he replied, then added, "It is often necessary to assist in certain matters. Sir Laughton has proven himself to be not only a valued partner in certain legal entanglements, but a worthy partner whom I have counted upon on behalf of certain clients in the past.

"You understand that I cannot share their names or the circumstances. Let us simply say that we both work for justice and continued peace in very difficult situations, and have relied on each other and the other person's integrity in the past. And it is not that I do not understand that certain matters are most critical."

I was certain that was as much of an honest response that we could hope for. It appeared that Brodie was of the same opinion.

"We have followed certain information that has led us to Frankfurt," he began. "And two names of persons who are involved."

He then told Herr Wagner what we had learned about Szábo and a possible connection to a man by the name of Bruhl.

"Sebastian Bruhl," he replied. "Both men are known in certain circles, although Bruhl has never been seen and there are those who doubt his existence." He rose from behind his desk.

"Perhaps you would join me in refreshment after your long trip."

I looked over at Brodie with some surprise.

"Of course," he replied.

"Come then, I know of an excellent place."

When the attendant in his office had suggested the driver for the firm, Herr Wagner had simply replied, "We will walk, it is a good weather."

However, once beyond the entrance to his office building, Herr Wagner waived down a street-hired coachman.

I looked over at Brodie in question at the somewhat odd behavior.

When the driver pulled to the curb, we climbed aboard. Herr Wagner settled himself across from us.

"It is often best to be discreet in certain matters, would you not say, Herr Brodie?"

That excellent place was the Hotel Frankfurt, a well-known international hotel with its five-story wings in the classic style, a wide sidewalk where carriages queued in a line, bold arched entrance, and flowers at each balcony in spite of the changing season. We were greeted by the concierge in English as well as German.

The restaurant at the Hotel Frankfurt was filled with guests even at this time in the later afternoon. I overheard conversations in German, of course, along with French, English, and Italian. A reminder that Frankfurt was an international center for industry and commerce, as well as banking.

"It is often best to lose oneself in a crowd," Herr Wagner commented as we arrived at a table in one of several alcoves with potted plants set about, and with a wall behind.

It very much reminded me of Brodie's habit in public places, pubs, taverns, and other restaurants about London. Most interesting, I thought.

It was an insight that added to Sir Laughton's recommendation of the man. He obviously chose to be discreet—losing ourselves in a crowd where no one would know us or pay any attention.

He ordered wine, instead of the beer I had expected. It was a white wine, with a hint of fruit as I lifted my glass that had been chilled.

"The wine, an investment on my part that has been most lucrative," he explained. "And now, we may speak freely."

Over the next two hours, Brodie explained as much as he chose to reveal about the stolen documents, the murder of Sir Collingwood, and the apparent involvement of Angeline Cotillard on behalf of the man who was rumored to be her lover. He included our encounter the day before at the museum in Brussels.

"We also have information that Szábo may be working with the man, Bruhl."

Herr Wagner nodded, then waited until the waiter who had returned filled our wine glasses once more. There was a brief conversation in German, to which Herr Wagner replied, "*Bitte.*"

A second bottle of wine appeared, and we exchanged pleasantries about the weather until he left.

"Both of these men are very enterprising. The first man you mentioned is known to local authorities, however he has managed to elude capture or has provided substantial compensation for certain people to look the other way."

He looked at Brodie now. "There is an underground economy in most cities that operates independently of the establishment, for a fee. This man is known to participate in the acquisition of certain items, artifacts, currency, and...perhaps documents, which he then makes available to clients."

He made it sound like any vendor or typical businessman.

"He would be in a position to make certain things available to the second man you mentioned, who has no country he calls his own, no loyalty to anyone, and has been known to leave a potential customer without his purse and the item he attempted to purchase over some slight. A very dangerous man."

"How does he go about contacting potential purchasers?" I asked.

"The first gentleman Mr. Brodie spoke of has a list of past clients that he might contact if a certain item of value came available. He would put out the word as any businessman might.

"He has been known to place an item of importance or historic value with the auction house. He then has the 'house' make it known that certain 'rare' items will be made available, and his clients respond by attending the auction. The other *gentleman*," he did use the term with certain disdain, "he has been known to make 'purchases' through a proxy. It is all seen as quite normal. The first gentleman receives a small reward for making the item available, the item is then 'offered' by the other man you have inquired about, to other parties for the highest bidder."

"It sounds as if the auctions occur quite regularly," I commented.

"We live in precarious times, Lady Forsythe. Interesting but precarious. And then there are the private auctions by invitation only."

There was no need to ask who potential purchasers might be for those documents. It could well include any foreign government, as well as someone in a high position within the German government.

"There is also the woman, Angeline Cotillard," I reminded him.

"Yes, the actress. A convenient '*profession*.'" This was added with a certain sarcasm.

"It would certainly allow her to travel to most any large city, as well as provide access to others in positions of authority."

"She travels with a small, but verra dangerous man," Brodie added.

Wagner nodded. "There are those who know far more about these things."

"Those who operate in the underground," I presumed. It did seem that he knew quite a bit about that.

He nodded over another sip of wine.

"In my profession, I have crossed paths with many people. This other gentleman, Bruhl," again there was that hint of cynicism. "You must understand, he gives a great deal of money to the poor, not only here but in other places. He is seen as much like your Robin Hood, and there are those who would protect him even though no one has ever seen him."

I understood his meaning. "And he perhaps supports an element of unrest among certain groups as well?" I suggested.

"Perhaps," he replied.

"I have traveled and seen such things, sir," I explained. "The *gentleman*, as you call him, has the blood of innocent people on his hands."

He nodded. "Intelligent as well as beautiful. You participate in a dangerous business, Lady Forsythe."

It was not a threat, and I didn't take it as such.

"Then you will be able to assist us?"

"I will make contact with people I know," he replied, then inquired, "Do you have accommodations for your stay in our city?"

Seventeen

IT WAS ARRANGED for him to contact us at the hotel. From there we could use their telegram services back to London as well.

"Do you trust him?" I asked Brodie after we reached our room.

"I trust Sir Laughton," he replied of my great-aunt's lawyer who had intervened on his behalf in the past, with no less than Sir Avery.

"We will see what he is able to learn from those he knows," he added, but I knew there was more.

"And?"

"A man who wants something can be verra motivated."

"Such as?"

"A man who wants to join his family."

That wasn't difficult to determine.

"Karl Schneider." Schmidt's brother-in-law.

Brodie nodded. "He may not be able to help, however it's always good to have another source for information just to be certain."

Most particularly in a place where he didn't have his usual resources, I thought. And then there was that experience from his time with the MET.

I was starving. "I'll work on my notes and then order up supper."

"Aye, best to keep here until we have word from Wagner," he replied. "With the cost of the room, I can only imagine what supper will be."

Spoken like a true Scot. That reputation for thriftiness was well deserved.

"You needn't worry about the additional expense," I told him.

"I canna imagine that Sir Avery will be forthcoming?"

"Most hotels in large cities have the ability to make banking available for their guests. I've used such arrangements in the past."

There was a frown. "Ye know I dinna want ye using yer own funds. I can handle the expenses over what Sir Avery provided."

I was aware of that. "Nevertheless. You may repay me when we return to London."

He made that typically Scottish sound as he left the room, the door snapping shut after him.

I took advantage of running water in the adjoining bathroom, then dressed once more, and went to the writing desk in the sitting room.

Brodie and supper arrived very near the same time. I waited to inquire if there was any word from either Herr Wagner or Karl Schneider until after the hotel attendant had gone.

I had given the man compensation for bringing supper in a timely manner. It was a habit learned from my great-aunt.

"*If you compensate them additional, they will be certain to*

A DEADLY SCANDAL

provide excellent service. It is also well-known that if you provide additional compensation to the hotel manager it will rarely find its way into the hands of those who have provided the extra service."

Words of wisdom from a world traveler in her younger years.

"What is it?"

He did have that way of reading me, as he called it. I was still working on that where he was concerned.

"Something..." I replied, which told him nothing. It wasn't something I could put my finger on. "Something in his manner..."

"Yer woman's intuition?" he asked, removing a domed lid from one of the plates at the table.

"He seemed somewhat...curious. Almost too attentive, which is most unusual for wait staff." I tried to explain what I had glimpsed for just a moment. Out of habit I had closed my notebook when he arrived.

I had ordered up traditional Frankfurt fare with potatoes, fresh bread, apple tarts, and wine made from currants and blackberries.

Brodie eyed the typical Frankfurt fare suspiciously. "What the devil is that?"

I glanced down at the somewhat over-proportioned sausages on the platter.

"It looks like somethin' I might not want to eat."

"Such as?" I couldn't imagine this from someone with his background on the street.

"It looks verra much like what one might find in a butcher shop when the man goes about cutting up the beast."

I gave that some thought. "Not intestines for certain. I've seen those in the meat markets."

209

"Ye know wot I'm speakin' of, the parts of the male animal. I canna eat such a thing. It looks like..."

"Such as?" I asked with wide-eyed innocence as I skewered one of the sausages, deposited it on my plate, then proceeded to slice it and took a bite.

"Oh, my," I exclaimed.

That dark gaze narrowed on me.

"It's quite excellent," I replied. "And the potatoes as well, in a cream and onion sauce. However, if you choose not to eat..."

He pulled the opposite chair out from the table and sat rather abruptly, still glaring at me. He then proceeded to take one of the sausages along with potatoes onto his plate, and began to eat. However, not without a thorough examination of the sausage.

I did however notice the slight surprise on his face as he sliced off a portion of the sausage and ate it. It did seem that it was possible to teach an old dog new tricks, or a stubborn, temperamental Scot.

We finished the wine while I read over my notes to make certain that I hadn't forgotten anything.

"Did you also send off a message to Herr Schneider?"

"I placed a telephone call to the postal office to get a message to him. It is not far; however, it is unknown when it may be delivered. I simply told him that we had arrived and he could contact us here."

At a sudden knock on the sitting room door, Brodie looked over at me. I noticed his hand going to the inside of his coat as he went to answer it.

It was one of the hotel valets. He handed an envelope to Brodie.

Brodie closed the door, then slipped a knife under the sealed edge and opened it.

"Herr Wagner has made contact with the person he knows who may be able to assist. He hopes to have word in the morning."

He threw the note down onto the table. It was obvious that he was frustrated and not at all pleased with the arrangement.

Brodie was accustomed to using his own sources or searching for information on his own. But this was different. We were in a strange city, forced to rely on others with no way of knowing who we could trust. I shared his frustration.

"I'm going for a walk," he announced in a way that suggested he wanted to do it alone.

"Very well," I replied. "I will have the valet remove the service for our supper and have him bring up an English print paper."

I pushed back the urge to tell him to take care. He would not have appreciated it. Yet, there was that twinge of uncertainty. I had no one to call on here if something should go wrong.

He bent over me at the table and tilted my head up. "Ye have the revolver if there should be any difficulty while I'm gone."

I assured him that I did. He kissed me then.

"Lock the door after and dinna open it for anyone."

"Anyone?" I asked, although I knew his meaning.

He kissed me again. "*Caileag ghrinn*." And then kissed me lightly once more. "Ye are a cheeky lass."

"I do try."

I waited until he had gone, then made a call to the hotel front desk to request the valet, and requested that he bring the most recent issue of the English print newspaper.

It was over two hours later when Brodie returned. There

had been a light rain and his jacket was soaked, along with that dark hair. As I helped him off with his jacket and then laid it over a chair to dry, he eyed the newspaper that I had been reading at the table.

"The scandal pages?" he commented as I poured a glass of wine and handed it to him.

"Entertaining in the least," I replied. "And occasionally one can learn some interesting bit of gossip. My great-aunt never misses an issue in London. She knows far more scandalous things than the newspapers reveal as she is acquainted with just about everybody, dead or alive."

"The advantage of living a long time," he replied as he loosened the collar of his shirt.

"What did you discover while you were out and about?"

"There are at least six entrances and exits to the various parts of the hotel, including a separate entrance to the restaurant behind the server's station. There are four service areas at the back of the hotel as one would expect for a place this size, and there are four more lifts in the East wing once one passes past the banquet hall.

"There is a coach entrance at each end of the hotel in addition to the main entrance, one for each wing where guests may come and go."

"Are you anticipating that we might need to make an unexpected departure?"

That dark gaze fastened on me. "We are strangers here. Ye have learned well enough that certain people will do whatever is necessary to accomplish what they set out to do. We are relying on a man we don't know except by Sir Laughton's word." He took a sip of wine. "Two people have already been murdered and yerself attacked. It is safe to assume they know who we are and that we're here. It is a verra dangerous situation."

I waited for what he would usually have said next, that he didn't want me there, or in the least that we needed to return to London and let everything fall where it may, or the distinct possibility that he would attempt to send me off by myself, definitely not a good option with an outcome that might very well get him killed.

I was fully prepared for any of those possibilities. However, there was no ultimatum, no over-bearing Scot's temper.

"We need to be careful, and most clever," he added.

I understood being careful. It was the latter that intrigued me.

"What do you suggest?"

"You told me earlier that you can arrange for funds through the hotel. How much might you be able to arrange?"

This was most intriguing.

I knew that Brodie earned enough from his inquiry cases to cover the rent on the office at the Strand and other related expenses. Two of our recent cases had been particularly lucrative, one of them on behalf of the Crown. I had never questioned what he did with his compensation, just as he had never inquired about my resources.

I did have investments that our great-aunt had made for both me and my sister. There had been 'gifts' as she called them from time to time, on our birthdays and Christmas holidays.

"*Always remember, my dears, that money is power,*" she had explained to both of us. "*Particularly for a woman. I have a great deal of it, more than the Queen, and one day that will all go to you and your sister, and the investments I've made on your behalf will make both of you quite wealthy all over again.*"

It was comforting to know, as well as a great responsibility. As far as '*one day,*' I did hope that was a long way off. In the mean time we had our occasional gifts, and I had the royalties from my books which had been magnificently successful.

Returning to Brodie's question, "That would depend on the banks, London to Frankfurt. At least fifty..."

He nodded that frown deepening. "Fifty pounds."

"Fifty thousand pounds," I replied. "More or less, the last time I met with my banker. There are the expenses for the town house, and the regular amount that he sends to the London Charity Home for Children."

"Fifty thousand?" He choked on his wine.

I nodded. "It might be a bit less, but very near that. Are you quite all right?"

"Fifty thousand pounds," he repeated, slowly recovering.

"Of course, there are also bonds and certificates of investment, but those are not easily converted."

He stared at me. "Fifty thousand pounds. There are people who never see that much in a lifetime, who can hardly imagine that much."

I refused to apologize. In fact, saw nothing to apologize for.

"There were gifts from my great-aunt over the years," I explained. "However, the rest I have earned from my books," I emphasized, since he seemed to be having some difficulty. "And I have saved most of it, after..."

"Yer father," he commented, from what I had told him in the past about myself. And there was more, of course, that he had no doubt learned from my great-aunt.

"I promised myself, that I would always be able to take care of Linnie and myself, that I would never be dependent on anyone ever again."

"And ye have done that, lass, and more. God knows, I could never fault ye for yer reasons."

He leaned toward me and took my hands in his. "The most

I earned as a police inspector with the MET before I left was three pounds seven shillings a week."

"You did it for the money, of course."

There was a quick flash of a smile at one corner of his mouth. "Of course. And some sort of need to help others because I knew that I could. To see things set right in some small way."

And he had with the cases he took on, some of which paid very little, if anything. His way of giving back.

"Do you have a plan?"

"Perhaps. We will need to see what Herr Wagner is able to learn."

His hands tightened around mine. He shook his head.

"It could be dangerous."

What a surprise, considering what had already happened.

"Ye are more important to me than my life."

When I would have replied, he shook his head. "Ye must let me say it."

And when I didn't interrupt further...

"I understand verra well that ye are an independent woman. I suppose I wouldna have ye any other way." He brushed my cheek with his fingers. "Bein' with ye is never unin-teresting, to say the least. But here, in this place and this case, it may become necessary to buy our way out of here. I would have yer promise that ye will do as I ask until this is done. If I ask ye to leave, that ye will."

I wanted to protest, to argue that the two of us in this situ-ation were better than one by himself. After everything we'd said to one another, he was not ordering me. He was asking. It was a reminder of things I had forgotten in my anger. And he had said it, that I was more important to him than his own life.

I did understand, and it was easier that I thought it would be.

However...

"And if I ask you to leave, you will do so," I replied. "I would have your promise."

There was no argument. Instead, he pulled me to him and kissed me quite thoroughly.

I was wakened as Brodie moved about the room. It was quite early, light barely there at the edge of the drapes covering the windows, his shadow moving about as he found his trousers, then his boots. With a soft curse he looked for his shirt, a hand going back through that dark hair in frustration.

"On the floor by the armoire." I remembered where I had last seen it. "That will teach you to hastily leave your clothes lying about."

He apparently found his shirt, then returned to the bed, his shadow with those wide shoulders and the darker shadow of the fine dark hair on his chest. He bent and kissed me.

"And it's seems ye left yer knickers on the floor as well, lass."

"Whatever will the staff think?"

He stood abruptly. "It seems the staff have arrived." He pulled on his shirt, then left the bedroom. I heard the sound as the door opened to the sitting room, and a brief exchange of conversation.

Brodie returned. "We are to meet with Herr Wagner in the main restaurant in one hour." He looked at me as I left the bed.

"Have I told ye that I like yer hair down like that?"

And...without my knickers.

. . .

"The man I made contact with is a...client," Herr Wagner explained. "He has many diverse business dealings."

"Including transactions with Szábo from time to time," Brodie concluded.

"Where there is money to be made, Herr Brodie. You are a man of experience in these things as I understand, from your time with the London Police, and perhaps with your private inquiries on behalf of certain clients."

"Go on," Brodie replied.

"There are rumors among certain people about a valuable item that has recently become available."

Certain people? I wondered if he was perhaps protecting that client. Szábo perhaps? It was possible, though he had never mentioned the name of his client. And now? What could we believe?"

"The documents we spoke of," Brodie clarified.

"You must understand, this is a very dangerous situation, the information that was shared with me," he continued. "There are three interested parties so far, with more anticipated by tomorrow night for the 'auction' that is to be held."

"What of Bruhl?" Brodie asked. "Is he part of this?"

"He will never participate directly. He will always have someone who will participate on his behalf."

"What is the floor for the auction for this 'valuable item?'" I had some knowledge of how they usually worked from attending auctions with my great-aunt, when a certain item that had found its way from the family into other hands. A sword of Sir William came to mind—her ancestor, William the Conqueror.

The sword had been authenticated by an expert in such

weapons, and there was a detailed description in family archives. In the end, after some very fierce bidding my great-aunt had the winning bid. The sword now hung in the weapons gallery at Sussex Square.

"By all accounts, Sir William was quite ruthless. My grand-father had a journal supposedly kept by the monk who traveled with him. The London Museum has been trying to get their hands on it for years.

"The Normans put such importance in the number of bodies in a campaign. As I said, quite ruthless. And in the end William conquered Britain," my great-aunt added. *"I thought it important to restore the sword to the family. You or Linnie will inherit all of these things one day."*

My sister wanted nothing to do with ancestral weapons. We did have quite a bloody history. However, Lily was now party of the family.

"It's a grand sword," she had declared when she first saw it. *"How many people do ye think he might have killed?"*

Yes, well, I had emphasized that we lived in a far more civilized world now. She had looked at me with an expression I had come to know quite well.

And now? I thought. Certain parties in this civilized world were apparently gathering like vultures eager to obtain the spoils of someone's vision for the future.

From where I was, it was not encouraging for man's future.

Power and greed, my great-aunt once commented. *"You will come to understand it better with your travels."*

I had. And that was part of the reason I was here now with Brodie. I had no idea what Sir Collingwood's motive was in giving the plans to Angeline. Perhaps we never would. And I suspected that it wasn't as if we could stop progress, other countries developing the same sort of things.

However, we were here, and we hoped to stop this. At the moment that prospect wasn't encouraging.

I did wonder what we might hope to do at this point. Steal back the documents, if, in fact, someone hadn't already copied them with the hope of profit for themselves?

That would require finding out who presently had them and where they were. Problem number one.

Most certainly Angeline or Szábo, or whoever was acting on their behalf, was experienced in these things and would take all necessary precautions to protect their investment.

Problem Number Two—If we were able to get past Problem Number One, it would be getting out of Frankfurt. The only assurance when it came to this was that the people involved would not be contacting the police—*if* we were able to retrieve the documents, which brought us back to Problem Number One.

It was really quite obvious. In a way, Brodie had struck upon a possible solution perhaps without realizing it.

In spite of everything, or perhaps because of it, there was no time to discuss what I was about to propose if the auction between different factions was to take place. And those documents would disappear with the buyer.

"You will need to let those organizing the auction know that there will be another party participating, Herr Wagner," I announced at the same time I ignored the questioning look from Brodie.

Herr Wagner looked at me with a mixture of surprise and interest which did make me wonder if he was involved in this somehow. Perhaps an attorney's fee?

While I had the deepest respect for Sir Laughton, my great-aunt's attorney, in view of the difficult situations he had handled on behalf of Brodie, my great-aunt had confided that there were instances in the past where he had perhaps—emphasis on the word *perhaps*—manipulated the law from time to time on behalf of a client.

I did not inquire who that client might have been. I did suppose that anyone who was educated in the law might be able to find certain details that might favor a situation.

As for here and now, we had only Herr Wagner to rely upon and no knowledge of German laws. In consideration of that it did seem that we were forced to take extreme measures.

Herr Wagner studied me with growing curiosity.

"Who would that be, Lady Forsythe? Do you represent someone who would want to be included in the auction? I do not know if that is possible."

"I wish to be included, Herr Wagner," I announced and ignored Brodie's not quite subtle reaction, the expression on his face, and the way he suddenly sat forward at his chair.

"That would be most...unusual, Lady Forsythe."

"Because I am a woman?" I thought of Angeline Cotillard who was somehow involved in all of this. Another woman, and I was not about to be set aside.

"It is not that," he replied. "You are here investigating the murder of the very man who apparently was responsible for handing over the documents."

"The murder, yes. But let us speak plainly, Herr Wagner. You have said that the auction will be attended by those who represent other governments and with the means to participate."

"Please continue," he replied.

"Mr. Brodie and I represent an interested party, the British government. And I assure you that I have the means to participate."

"Most interesting. If I understand correctly, you propose to join the auction with the purpose of securing the winning bid. Is that correct?"

"It is."

"Do you understand that this 'auction' might very well reach the equivalent of several thousand of your English pounds if you were to bid recklessly? And the consequences for that?"

"I am quite familiar with the process of auctions, and I have access to sufficient funds to participate on a level with any of the other...participants."

Herr Wagner sat back in his chair, chin resting on his steepled fingers. "My good friend, Sir Laughton, said that you and Mr. Brodie were remarkable, if somewhat unusual partners." He was thoughtful for several moments. "I would need to speak with my 'client' in this matter, you understand."

"Of course," I replied, then added, "There would also be a substantial fee for your participation." I caught the interest in his gaze.

For his part, Brodie remained silent, something that undoubtedly would not last when we were finally alone.

"I understand that each of the participants are required to post an amount with the gentleman who is in charge of the auction. An assurance of each person's participation."

"Of course," I replied. "You have only to let me know what that amount would be."

"Insane!" Brodie declared after we left our meeting with Herr Wagner with his promise that he would leave word when he was able to contact his 'client' with my proposal.

Brodie shook his head. "And at the same time, it's most brilliant, foolish, reckless. I have reason to question if there is any insanity in yer family. Perhaps a long-lost relation consigned to Bedlam!"

I was somewhat familiar with the hospital in Bromley, Bethlem Royal Hospital, that had been given that nickname.

"Not anyone that I'm aware of," I replied. "If it works and I'm allowed to join the auction, it is quite brilliant."

"Just how do ye propose to accomplish this?"

"The same as everyone who will be participating. I will post the amount required and then enter the bidding process."

"Ye do realize there will be all sorts of unknown persons also there, to protect others bidding, including Szábo and others just like him."

"That is the reason that you will be there."

"Bedlam," he repeated. "If ye dinna have family who have been there, ye may be the first. If we survive this."

Eighteen

"**THERE IS** every possibility that Herr Wagner's proposal to the others who will be participating may very well send someone to take care of the 'matter' before the auction takes place," Brodie continued as we went to the hotel front desk.

He was handed a message.

By that I assumed he meant that we might expect a 'visitor in the night.' To eliminate the competition.

"What is it?" I asked at the change of expression on his face that I had seen countless times. It was his 'police inspector' expression which might have meant anything.

He thanked the desk manager, then took my arm.

"There is a man waiting for us in the hotel café."

There had hardly been enough time for Herr Wagner to contact his client in the matter we had discussed, and it did seem unlikely that if he had someone sent to eliminate the competition, as it were, he would hardly select a hotel coffee shop to do the deed.

"Until we know what this is about yer to wait here," Brodie told me just inside the entrance to the café.

I agreed as I looked around for who the man might be who had left that note at the hotel front desk.

There were several couples seated at tables with their morning coffee and breakfast, a single gentleman who was dressed quite formally in a coat and trousers, and another man, somewhat young, seated by himself who wore the usual clothes of someone who had traveled a distance with a short coat, trousers, and cap, and a worn satchel on the floor.

As Brodie crossed the floor, the man stood and greetings were exchanged. He was almost as tall as Brodie, but quite robust with wide shoulders beneath the coat, a butcher by profession, Schmidt had told us. Brodie turned and motioned for me to join them.

"This is Karl Schneider," he made the introduction.

The man appeared to be no more than twenty-five or thirty years old with pleasant features, brown hair and brown eyes. He nodded, greeting us in heavily accented English with a broad smile.

"I am here," he announced, which was somewhat amusing. "I am most pleased to meet you. My sister sent a telegram. You will take me to England, after some business that brought you here. *Ja?*"

Brodie nodded. "Aye, if you can help us with a certain matter."

Schneider nodded. "I will help in any way, Herr Brodie, if it means that I can go to your country."

I knew precisely what Brodie was doing...not precisely, but with a fairly good idea as we returned to our suite with Karl Schneider. Quid pro quo.

If Herr Schneider would help us, we would help him leave Frankfurt. If we survived.

Over the next few hours, Brodie explained as much as he

could. At the same time, I watched as he exchanged comments with Schneider, putting him at ease at the same time drawing on his expertise from working with the MET, encountering all sorts in his investigations there, and from the streets.

"People are no different one place to another," he had once explained the difference between those he knew in Edinburgh and London, and those we had encountered in Paris in a previous inquiry case.

"The same purpose drives most people—a roof over the head, food in the stomach, a safe place, survival in places that are not safe. It is like the hound," he had provided an example.

"He does what he needs to survive on the streets, aside from the food ye give him. Ye have seen the disgusting things he returns with from time to time. He prefers the alcove at the office when the weather sets in and will defend it to the death. It is much the same with a good many men and women.

"And I have found there is often more honesty with the criminal sort than others. At least ye know exactly what they are about."

While it seemed most likely that Karl Schneider was not the criminal sort, considering the ease with which they spoke now, and the fact that Brodie had brought him to our room, it was also very obvious that the man was determined to do whatever was necessary to make certain he was able to go to his family in London.

"Herr Schmidt spoke of some things that prevented ye from traveling there before now," Brodie commented. "I would know what those things are if we are to assist ye."

Schneider hesitated. "You are with the London Police?"

"Not for some time," Brodie assured him. "I handle private inquiry cases now, the reason we were sent, so as not to involve the German authorities."

"You work together?" Schneider asked.

"Lady Forsythe is my partner, and that is all you need to know."

Our guest looked over at me. "My sister's husband spoke of this in his earlier telegram. You are familiar with the sword, *ja*?"

I nodded. It seemed that Herr Schmidt had shared a great deal with his wife's brother.

Schneider grinned. "I am good with the blade as well in my work." He opened the satchel and retrieved a rather nasty-looking knife.

"I have my tools so that I can find work in London. And this. I keep it very sharp. It is good to be able to protect oneself."

Very much so, I thought.

I did like him, however deferred to Brodie with his greater experience in such matters. It seemed that he had made a decision.

"Ye will do," Brodie told him. "Now, for what lies ahead if all goes accordin' to plan. So that we may all leave."

Brodie explained that we were waiting to hear about a 'transaction' that was to take place by way of an auction. He then inquired what Schneider knew about Szábo.

"If the rumors are true, he is most *dangerous*," the one word he used to describe him, then explained. "He is Hungarian, not German." He almost spat out the words.

"Not a man to be trusted. He has killed many, but the bodies are never found. They disappear, even rumors of the *Polizeidirektor* here. They look the other way when it is to their advantage. And there are other stories about things he has done in France, and England. Always for money, a great deal of money." He looked from me to Brodie.

"Is he to be part of the auction?"

"He is responsible for the item that is to be auctioned to the highest bidder."

Schneider looked at me. "This is very dangerous for a woman."

"She will be participating in the auction, if we receive word that the others are acceptable to the idea," Brodie explained.

"Ah!" Schneider exclaimed and laid the knife down on the table. "She will need protection." He looked at Brodie.

"You should not stay here. If one man knows you are here, others will know."

It was obvious that Brodie had thought of that.

"Ye know of a place?"

Schneider nodded. "It is not far, where I have made deliveries in the district." There was a look over at me.

"It is not as fine as the hotel, but it is clean and safe. You can get your messages here while we plan what is to be done."

It seemed that we had taken on a partner, or at least an associate who was quite willing to do whatever was necessary to guarantee his passage to England.

Schneider waited just outside the hotel entrance while we packed our few pieces of clothing.

As for the room, Brodie told me to leave it as it was. Our breakfast service had been collected with fresh linens and soaps provided in the adjoining bathroom.

The reservation had been left open as we had no way of knowing how long we might need to remain in Frankfurt. As far as anyone else might be concerned, we were still there or soon to return.

On our way to meet with Herr Schneider, Brodie stopped at the front desk and informed the clerk that we did not wish to be disturbed in our room, and that he would be returning to the desk from time to time to inquire about any messages.

With that we left the hotel.

The *'residenschloss'* where Schneider made his weekly deliveries was in the same district, however, off the main city center from the hotel, where those not of the means to stay in the hotel could still afford to stay in the city.

It was a two-story former private residence of some city official in the medieval period, with an arched entrance and a round corner tower above the second story. Over the entrance were a pair of carved plaster lions supporting a crown.

"These are good people," Schneider assured us as the driver departed.

We were greeted inside the residence by a stout woman with her hair tucked under a scarf, bright color on her cheeks, and a bucket and mop in her hands.

She smiled broadly as she greeted Karl.

"My friends," he explained. "We need two rooms."

She nodded and there was a brief conversation in German, then a smile as she rounded a narrow counter that looked as if it might be as old as the residence, and produced two room keys.

"I have known her and her husband for several years. She will say nothing if anyone should ask," Karl assured us as we climbed the narrow stone steps to the second floor.

The two rooms were across from each other in the old house.

The walls were stone with an arched window that looked out on the street below. Wide dark timbers made up the floor. The furnishings were of dark wood as well, a simple table and chairs.

The bed against the wall was quite high, made of that same dark timber with thick bedding, and I did wonder who might have slept in it.

"He did say that she kept a verra clean house," Brodie reminded me.

That was some reassurance that there wouldn't be more than the two of us in that bed.

The waiting for some word from Herr Wagner, that I would be allowed to participate in the auction of the documents, seemed interminable.

As I waited in the common room downstairs, Frau Meier, the proprietress of the house, inquired if I had any laundry that needed washing. I provided her a shirt and socks of Brodie's, along with a shirtwaist of mine.

In broken English, she inquired if I had any additional clothing items with something that sounded very much like 'underthings.'

I assured her that I would wash them myself. She retreated with Brodie's socks and the shirts, and a definite sniff as if she was insulted.

I had only my shift and my slip which was much the worse for wear after using a portion of it to bandage poor Alex.

As for other 'underthings,' I rarely wore pantaloons as they were far too bulky and cumbersome. Brodie seemed to appreciate it.

"*Has anyone ever told ye that ye are a wanton wench.*"

"*Only yourself,*" I had replied. "*No one else would ever be the wiser, as I do not have a maid, and I most certainly do not lift my skirts for just anyone.*"

That had promptly ended the conversation in a most interesting way as we were in my great-aunt's private coach at the time.

Now we waited, and continued to wait.

Herr Schneider was most entertaining with stories that I only half understood. It did seem that he had led a most interesting life with an assortment of 'professions,' some which brought him into disagreement with the authorities.

He had taken the advice of his sister, or possibly by threat, that he needed to mend his ways if he hoped to be allowed to join them in England. That led to his training with a local butcher in his district who had known the family.

He made a decent living and there was the promise of taking over the business when the owner could no longer work. However, as he pointed out, that might be another twenty years. And there was always the threat of the authorities that hung over his head.

I didn't inquire what the crimes were. It was possibly best not to know.

Brodie went back to the Hotel Frankfurt midafternoon to inquire about messages, however, there was no word from Herr Wagner. As the hours passed, it did seem as if our scheme might not have been acceptable to the other parties who were to participate in the auction.

"Any word?" I inquired when he returned once more from the hotel very near nine o'clock in the evening. Yet, I could tell the answer by the expression on his face.

"It is possible that we may be forced to return to London empty-handed."

We were alone in our room after a simple late meal of sausage and potatoes.

"If we are not successful in gaining entrance to the auction, it will go on as planned with the documents sold to the highest bidder and they will disappear."

To be used for heaven knew what purpose.

Sir Avery had explained the possible consequences in one of our last meetings before leaving London. Those documents had the potential to advance the possibility of a war with devastating consequences.

"Go to bed," Brodie eventually told me when it was very near midnight. "There is nothing more to be done tonight. I will be in the common room below with Herr Schneider. There are things to discuss."

I could only imagine what those might be, considering the danger we could be facing.

"Do you trust him?"

"We are forced to, if this plan comes together."

I washed in the guest's bathroom in the hall after he left, then returned to our room. There was no need of a fire on the stone hearth as it was not cold. I slept little, waking from time to time as one does in strange places to discover that Brodie had not yet returned.

It was quite late when I heard the door open. I had discovered the electric in the room earlier, but he didn't turn it on. Instead, he undressed in the dark, then climbed the small step up into the bed.

"Bloody hell!" I heard the exclamation as he eventually found me and pulled me against him as was his way, as if he thought I might slip away again. Not that I minded. It was most pleasant. Now particularly, so far from London.

"One could break their neck getting out of bed in a rush. And we're sinking into the damned thing."

"It's a down mattress, quite thick actually. I believe the idea is that you are not supposed to leave the bed until morning," I replied.

"Or ever," he replied. "It's a wonder yer ancestor lived through conquering Britain if the beds were like this."

"I'm told that he eventually returned to France. Perhaps the beds were larger and firmer there." Although, by our experience, they were much the same unless one was sleeping on the floor.

It hardly mattered. With everything that had been set in motion, we were both restless and unable to sleep. He eventually climbed out of the bed, and I listened drowsily as he rummaged around a bit. A match flared as he lit his pipe, and in the glow of that brief flame I glimpsed that dark gaze and those handsome, intense features.

Then he put the match out and there was only the faint glow as he sat on that chair before the darkened hearth and drew on the pipe, that fragrance floating in the still air inside the room.

I climbed out of the bed and crossed to him. His hand found mine in the darkness and he pulled me down on his lap. I laid my head on his shoulder, my hand on his chest.

We sat there for the longest time, his body warm against mine as the room chilled.

"Tomorrow..." he started to speak, barely more than a whisper.

I pressed my fingers against his lips. I knew what he was going to say, that it would be dangerous at best, perhaps even that he didn't want me part of it.

"Tomorrow is soon enough," I whispered, then bent his head toward me, finding him as I pressed my mouth against his, my fingers stroking through his beard.

He set the pipe aside, then stood, taking me back to the bed with him.

It was well after eight o'clock when we rose the next morning. Brodie dressed, then left to return to the hotel for any messages that might have come in since the last time he was there, while I shared breakfast with Karl in the common room.

When he returned, I knew immediately that he'd received a message. He handed it to me. It was from Herr Wagner.

He was finally able to meet late the night before with his client, who had reluctantly agreed for me to participate in the auction. It seemed that greed was great motivation.

Herr Wagner asked to meet with both of us as soon as possible as the 'event,' as he called it, was to begin at eight o'clock that evening at a private location that would only be disclosed just prior to beginning.

Before that could take place, a deposit of ten thousand in francs, marks, or English pounds was to be made with the director of the local auction house who had been retained to conduct the private auction.

"I sent a telegram to London last night," Brodie told me. "I explained what has happened and about the auction."

There was only one person he would have contacted. Sir Avery.

"There is no word as of this morning," he added.

I heard the unspoken in his voice, that we might not hear from him in time.

"Ye understand?"

"Then there is nothing else for us to do but continue as planned and then return to London."

I knew what he was thinking—*if* we returned to London.

"I never wanted this for ye."

"I know that, however here we are."

"This is not one of yer lady adventures to Egypt, or Hong Kong, or Budapest."

"It's not?" I replied. "I've always wanted to play some high-stakes game or bid at an auction for a priceless relic."

He glared at me. "I should tie ye up and ship ye back."

"Except for one thing, Mr. Brodie," I reminded him as I straightened his tie. "I'm the one they have approved to participate in the auction. And it is the only chance we have to obtain those documents."

He was not pleased, but he agreed. "Aye."

He slipped his arms around me and pulled me against him. "I thought I'd lost ye when ye left." He angled his head back so that I was forced to meet that dark gaze.

"I willna lose ye now, lass. Ye should know that I will do whatever is necessary to protect ye."

I knew what he was capable of. I had seen it in the past, and I shivered slightly. It was a promise, and he would kill to keep it.

I did hope it wouldn't come to that, yet I was not naïve. We were dealing with some very dangerous people who would also kill, and already had, for what they wanted. I needed to figure out how I was going to prevent him being killed.

Herr Wagner made arrangements for us to meet with the president of Deutsche Bank in Frankfurt.

There, I was able to arrange for funds to be transferred from my bank to the account of the auctioneer who was to oversee the evening's event, with the guarantee of full payment for the item being auctioned, when that was determined.

It was possible that I might be left penniless when it was all over.

"Do we know where the auction is to be held?" I asked as we left the bank with everything in place for the transfer of ten thousand pounds.

"Herr Wagner will let us know an hour before the time."

"Then it must be within the city," I concluded.

"My thought as well. That's the reason that I've given Karl

the task of purchasing three tickets on the late train leaving Frankfurt tonight."

It did seem that he was planning for all of us to survive the evening.

We returned to the *residenschloss* where we had spent the previous night. I did, after all, know Angus Brodie quite well.

"He could simply use those tickets and leave," I pointed out.

"Except for one thing. He needs our assistance legally to be able to enter England. Otherwise, he will find himself back here. Or worse."

Karl had already returned when we arrived. He handed the rail vouchers to Brodie who put them in a pocket inside his jacket.

We then spent the rest of the afternoon waiting to learn the location of the auction and planning, as best we could, the role each of us was to play in this very dangerous scheme.

Nineteen

WE HAD FINISHED supper in the common room of the Cober Haus, and continued to wait.

I was not good at waiting, although I had improved at that during our past inquiry cases. Brodie, however, gave no indication that he was impatient or frustrated.

The man I saw now was the one with over ten years' experience with the MET and several more in the cases he took for others—that almost unreadable expression, the way he went about our room as he carefully packed his valise and then suggested I do the same. It was obvious he was certain we would not be returning.

Then, as it grew later, that last trip back to the hotel to check for the message we were waiting for while I made certain I had packed everything into my travel bag, then paced about the room as thoughts crowded into my head.

Who would be there? Undoubtedly Szábo. Unless he sent someone on his behalf.

Why the delay? Certainly, everyone who was to participate

had arrived during the day, if not days earlier as word was sent out.

Had the auction been cancelled for some reason? Surely not with the potential for such high stakes.

Or, was it possible that we had been excluded after all?

When Brodie returned, I saw the answer to at least one of those questions in that dark gaze.

"It will begin in one hour," he told me, as Karl Schneider listened intently. "I have the location." Brodie showed the message from Wagner to him.

Karl nodded. "I know this place. It is not far, the old opera house that is to be torn down."

They had spoken at great length earlier after supper. Brodie had explained as much as he could, and made it clear that Karl's only opportunity depended on all of us getting on that last train tonight out of Frankfurt. If we failed in our efforts, so too would his chances to reach London.

"*What is worth taking so much risk?*" he had asked.

"Stolen documents, and two people have already been killed over the matter. More than that would be too dangerous for ye to know."

Karl nodded. "It is enough that you have come all this way. I do not need to know more. But I am going with you," he declared.

There was that infectious grin. "So that you do not come to harm."

Arrangements were then made for him to meet us at the Frankfurt Main rail station at midnight for the last departing train for the night.

Now, he watched as Brodie checked the revolver he always carried. I did the same with the smaller revolver that he insisted I carry.

"Ach!" Karl exclaimed, and then as if I was not in the room. "A woman with a gun? Does she know how to use it?"

"Of course," I replied, without going into the details of that first inquiry case. I then proceeded to open the breech, checked the cylinder of the five-shot pocket revolver, then snapped it shut.

"Aye," Brodie replied. "To prevent her taking mine."

Karl eyed me warily. "I will remember to stay behind you."

Brodie looked at me. "Ye have the weapon Munro gave ye?"

I lifted the hem of my skirt and showed him the blade I kept down the side of my boot.

"And she carries a knife?"

"I've only had to use it once," I explained. At the time it was for cutting away rope. I'd never had to use it on someone, and hoped I never would. The idea of being that close to someone threatening me was not a pleasant one.

Still, if necessary, I had learned some time ago that I had what Brodie called survivor instinct.

Brodie nodded, satisfied, as I returned the revolver to my travel bag.

"This could be verra dangerous," he told Karl. "There will be those there who are determined to have those documents."

Karl opened his bag and took out a butcher's cleaver. He proceeded to demonstrate, wielding it with amazing speed, then slamming it down on the table, the blade embedded in the wood.

"I prefer this."

"Good enough," Brodie told him. "I will remember to keep to your back as well."

Karl Schneider, the butcher, grinned.

• • •

As Karl had indicated, the theater was in the older part of the city, yet not far from the center of Frankfurt. The building looked to be at least three hundred years old with parapets, and I thought of William Shakespeare.

Before leaving the *residenschloss*, we had also rehearsed the roles we were to play during the forthcoming auction.

Obviously, I was to be the participant in the auction.

As for Brodie? It was safe to assume that those present would very well be aware of his role in attempting to retrieve the documents, and perhaps his former profession as a police detective with the MET. That might present a problem, although Herr Wagner hadn't mentioned anything of that sort.

The unknown part of it was whether any of them were aware that we'd been sent by Sir Avery of the Special Services after the murder of Sir Collingwood.

Angeline Cotillard was involved in that part of it. As was his way, Brodie chose to assume those there might be well informed regarding that, which would only increase the risk.

Then, there was Karl Schneider. It was very likely that no one present at the auction would know him. Brodie wanted him to remain behind yet close by, if possible.

If not...

Expect the unexpected.

I had learned that from him. It was something he had learned on the streets, and I knew from stories Munro had shared that it had kept them both alive in the past.

Brodie found a driver and the three of us entered the coach. He then gave him the destination of the old opera house.

The opera house was barely visible against the darkened skyline, except for the glow of lanterns at the entrance. As we left the coach, Karl departed, blending into the shadows along the front of the house.

The plan, as best we could make one, was for him to wait until the last coach arrived, then find his way inside and to the main part of the house where we presumed the auction was to take place.

A man waited just inside the entrance. He was a rough sort who spoke hardly any English, except to nod a vague acknowledgement as I gave my name. He then directed us to another man who escorted us to the main audience seating area. One of a set of double doors was opened and we entered the massive area.

I had seen other opera houses in Italy, with their elaborate seating, opera boxes that lined the walls, the stage hidden by massive, elegant velvet drapes with a double row of footlights and the orchestra pit just below. Not unlike the theater in London where my good friend Templeton performed.

Here the boxes were wrapped in darkness. No one would be listening to Verdi or Strauss as the players performed out their roles. No one would be waiting for those now-threadbare and torn velvet drapes to be drawn back as the first act began. As for the audience, there were barely enough chairs remaining, as it was perhaps the work of vandals.

There were, however, several chairs that had been arranged in a row much like at an auction house—a total of ten, I counted, with the orchestra director's stand placed before those rows. Not to conduct the orchestra, but to conduct the auction for those documents.

It was sad, I thought, that the grand old opera house should end this way, under the wrecking ball as I had once seen of an old building in London that stood in the midst of a newly planned roadway. Was this grand, sad old 'house' to make way for someone else's vision of an opera house? Or to make way for perhaps another rail line or street?

Brodie's hand tightened around my arm as he escorted me through the audience area toward the front of the house.

"Lady Forsythe," a man, who had now taken his place at the conductor's stand, commented in accented English.

"Englander," he added with a brief nod in our direction as Brodie escorted me to the last row of the seating that had obviously been placed for the auction, the better to see everyone he had explained as part of the 'plan,' and probably nearer the entrance.

A man stepped in front of Brodie and shook his head, his hand on Brodie's arm, in an unmistakable gesture that he was not to be allowed to remain for the auction.

I glanced at the others who had already arrived, each with at least one or two others who accompanied them, then caught the expression on Brodie's face.

He took hold of the man's wrist and I thought our efforts might end in the next moment.

To my surprise, the man let out a snarl then jerked his arm away, shaking his hand as he glared at Brodie.

I caught the nod from the auctioneer, and the man backed away.

"I thought certain he was going to force a confrontation and we were going to be sent away," I whispered. Or worse, I thought, considering what we knew about those present, and a great deal more we didn't know.

"It would have been difficult with no feeling in his hand," Brodie replied.

"How?"

"It's a simple thing if ye know the right place to apply pressure. I will show ye if we get out of here alive."

As it was, it hardly mattered, if we didn't. Not a pleasant thought.

It seemed we were the last to arrive of those who would be bidding in the auction. The auctioneer announced a handful of rules in German, and then in English, no doubt for my benefit.

However, I saw the acknowledgements from several of those present and then realized there were representatives from a handful of other countries.

He then described the item up for auction—documents recently acquired, and of great value, as described in the information each had previously received. A side door next to the orchestra pit opened and a wood chest was brought out by a statuesque woman with striking blonde hair and vivid lip color.

The resemblance to those paintings was unmistakable as was the lip color, found on that cigarette at Sandringham.

Angeline Cotillard made her entrance and deposited the carved wood chest on the table next to the auctioneer's stand. She then opened the lid and removed the thick roll of documents that had brought everyone here tonight.

The documents were authentic, the auctioneer assured everyone, acquired directly from the British Admiralty, revealing the development of an advanced weapon that could rain havoc down on other countries.

He then announced that surety deposits from all participants had been verified, and asked for the opening bid for the documents. Brodie's hand squeezed mine as it began.

Before we left Cober Haus I had explained the mechanics of an auction as well as the strategy.

"The strategy is to obtain the highest price," he had replied.

Yes, but there was more to it than that. It was very much like playing chess, I went onto explain. It was always best to wait, learn who your opponent or opponents were, and what they were willing to do. In this situation, what were they willing to bet in order to obtain the documents.

I thought of the telegram that I had sent before leaving the hotel for other accommodations and the response I had received, the message quite clear.

'You must do whatever is necessary for you and Mr. Brodie to safely return. I do wish I was there, however must consider Lily. You now have what you need. Do make it back in time to help plan the wedding.'

I had taken certain measures with the instructions I had then put in place at the hotel. All the same, I chose not to discuss the telegram or those arrangements with Brodie. He did have a penchant for insisting on keeping my family out of our work.

The bidding proceeded, quietly with a raised hand, from a man who spoke with a thick German accent, then another with a somewhat different accent. Prussian, I thought. Then there was a bid from a dark-complexioned man in a set of long robes who might be from one of the eastern countries.

The bid was then raised by a lean, unshaven man who spoke with a French accent. He was plainly dressed and accompanied by another man in the same clothes of a common worker.

"He is not French," I whispered to Brodie. "Possibly Hungarian by the accent."

Was he perhaps with one of the anarchist groups that had spread attacks across Europe the past several years?

It was difficult to imagine that he had access to the amount of money the bids had now reached. But there were rumors that the money to fund their activities to spread unrest in fact came from sources in growing industries who hid their identities to protect themselves.

It was horrifying to think it might be true.

And the purpose of the documents for the design of that air ship that everyone in that theater was desperate to obtain?

The bidding had reached very near fifty thousand pounds sterling. Let us see what the response would now be, I thought. I raised my hand.

Instead of the increments of five thousand pounds that we had been acknowledged by the auctioneer, I announced my own bid.

"One hundred thousand pounds sterling."

I immediately felt that dark gaze on me, along with several others in that ancient opera house.

"Do ye know wot ye are doin'?" Brodie whispered.

"Of course."

"But that kind of money...Ye dinnae have that much. They will expect payment."

I glanced over at him. "Trust me."

"I do, but this is dangerous."

"Yes, it is, but more so for those I have just outbid. Let us see what they are prepared to do."

The auctioneer repeated my bid. "One hundred thousand pounds?"

I nodded.

"You are prepared to pay that for the documents."

"I have access to sufficient funds...and more," I added, to stir the pot as Mrs. Ryan, my housekeeper was fond of saying.

"The funds are in a Swiss account, verified by the president of Deutsch Bank. I have written confirmation. I am certain that you will recognize the signature of the same man who has no doubt verified the funds of others present."

Brodie made that sound I had heard quite often. I saw his

hand slip inside the front of his jacket when there were no higher bids.

"You have a confirmation of the funds, Lady Forsythe?" The auctioneer called out.

I rose and approached the auctioneer's stand. I showed him the confirmation. When he would have taken it, I held it just out of reach.

"I'm certain you understand that my bank in Switzerland requires me to verify the final amount when the bank here in Frankfurt opens in the morning."

"I know her!" a voice cut through the tangle of conversations that had begun.

"They are working with the English authorities!"

I followed the sound of that voice and saw that short little man who had attacked me at the art exhibit in Brussels as he charged toward the auctioneer's stand.

It was no doubt a rash decision, not exactly part of the plan which had been for us to simply walk away with the documents at the conclusion of the auction. However, with that nasty little man charging toward me and Brodie at least twenty feet away...

I was not about to let that little man upend our case and the entire reason we were there. I had previously made the mistake of misjudging him because of his short height. I was not about to do that again and did what I should have done in Brussels.

I saw the blade he had in his hand, that he had used on Alex. Having encountered him before, I knew exactly what he would do when I swept his feet. As he reached me, I took a deep breath, swept his feet from under him. Only this time as he rolled and came to his feet, I had already pulled the revolver from my bag.

I pulled back the hammer as I had practiced hundreds of times at Brodie's insistence, and fired.

The shot caught the little man low at the shoulder as a scream came from the stage behind the auctioneer as a woman with blonde hair, and a glimpse of vivid red lip color ran down the steps with weapon in hand.

It could be none other than Angeline Cotillard.

I took advantage of that momentary shock that rippled through the bidders and grabbed the documents from the box at the table, stuffed the documents into my bag, then ran toward Brodie and the exit of the opera house.

"Ye might have told me wot ye were up to."

"I didn't know myself until that little fiend ran toward me."

He shoved me out the exit to the opera house where Karl Schneider suddenly appeared.

"Get her out of here. I'll meet ye at the rail station."

When I would have argued, he pulled me to him and kissed me hard.

"For once, do as yer told."

"What about you?" Shouts followed us from the opera house.

"I'll meet ye there."

"Brodie...!" I saw the look he gave Karl, and I suddenly knew exactly what was happening.

"I won't leave you!" I screamed at him.

He shook his head, and that dark gaze met mine.

"Go, now!"

He turned back and disappeared into the darkness as the light from a half dozen or more lanterns suddenly appeared and there was more gunfire.

Twenty

I FOUGHT AND I KICKED, and cursed. And discovered even with my training in the Far East, I was no match for a man as tall as Brodie but thicker of build, a butcher by trade, who was no doubt accustomed to handling carcasses of hogs and beef.

I was unable to throw a jab or my knee at him. I dropped my bag, however any attempt to sweep his feet was completely futile.

I continued to protest and curse, and managed to remind him that Brodie was the one who would be able to get him into England. All of it to no avail as he carried me, kicking and protesting, into the dark alleyway beside the opera house and threw me into the back of a wagon, the wood boards scraping my cheek.

How did he come by the wagon? Who did it belong to?

We had to wait for Brodie!

"A man I know in the city. He hauls things for people," he replied as he pushed me down into the bottom of the wagon that smelled suspiciously of animals, his knee at my back.

He grabbed one wrist then the other and bound my hands, then bound my ankles as I tried to kick out at him.

"We must go."

When I would have protested, he tied a cloth over my mouth and we left that part of the city...and Brodie.

The wagon eventually rolled to a stop. I tried to sit up, and felt a large hand at my shoulder pushing me back into the bottom of the wagon.

I caught the glow of a street lamp, and heard the familiar sounds of a train station, and knew we were quite nearby.

Brodie would be there. He had to be, however, instead of being released I was pinned once more in the bottom of the wagon. I was then rolled onto my side, a heavy carpet that smelled of grease and all sorts of other things thrown over me.

"It is best that no one sees you." Karl said. "I know these kinds of men. They will be looking for you. I am sorry. Do not struggle."

Do not struggle? I would have if it would do any good. It didn't. And where was my bag with those documents?

We knew almost nothing about Karl. We were taking it on faith that he was determined to reach England. How easy would it be for him to take the documents then sell them himself?

With that, unable to protest or defend myself, I was rolled again onto my other side, that carpet tucked around me in a tight cocoon that smothered my face.

It was hot and stifling inside the carpet as I was then hoisted once again over Karl's shoulder.

I was caught, trapped, and there was nothing I could do as I was jostled over his shoulder, barely able to breathe. I thought of the knife in my boot, impossible to reach. Yet the first chance I got...

He stopped, adjusting me in that stifling carpet on his shoulder as easily as he might have hoisted a carcass ready for the butcher's cleaver. I caught a muffled conversation in a mixture of German and English as I struggled to breathe.

"*Ja*, the baggage car for this," he told someone as he adjusted me over his shoulder.

I heard the sound of a heavy door rolled back. He clamped an arm around the rug, then continued a short way with some effort. We stopped again and he pulled the rolled carpet from his shoulder, and with a grunt of effort lowered that bundle with me trapped inside.

Were we in the baggage car?

There was a sharp slam of a heavy door, the distant sound of a train whistle muffled by that musty carpet, then a jarring motion as the train began to move.

No!

The tears came then, stinging at my eyes, then hot at my face and tight at my throat. I wanted to scream but couldn't as I lay there bound with that tight cloth over my mouth in that moldy rotting carpet.

Where was Brodie? Had Szábo and his people caught him?

There was a brief thought about that short man who had attacked me in Paris. Then it was gone as I thought of Brodie.

What would happen to him now? Was he even still alive?

I told him to trust me, and he had…The floor jolted and swayed beneath me as the train gradually picked up speed.

I tried to scream, choking on my tears, smothered by the heat inside the carpet.

After everything that had happened…

The air was knocked out of me as I was rolled over, the carpet coming loose about me. I was then rolled out into a disheveled pile at the floor of the lurching baggage car, the light from a nearby lantern almost painful.

The cloth was pushed down from my mouth. I cursed, but it was nothing more than a dry croak. My hair had come down and it was pushed back from my face. That dark gaze met mine.

"You need to take care, Herr Brodie" Karl warned. "She has a temper. She kicks like a mule, and I have never heard a woman curse like that."

"Aye," Brodie replied. "She does have a temper."

There was a great deal I wanted to say. Several curses came to mind as he pulled me against him, a hand going back through my tangled hair.

"Next time, ye need to tell me yer plans. Ye verra near got us both killed."

I was dirty from wherever that carpet had been before it was tossed in that wagon. My shirtwaist was torn from being hauled about by the butcher; my cheek throbbed. And the rope cut into my wrists.

"A hundred thousand pounds?" he then said, as he cut the rope with his knife. "Sir Avery? Something ye should have told me."

"Not Sir Avery," I finally managed to say as my voice returned. "I don't trust him after..."

I was about to say when he refused to help Brodie at first in that last inquiry case, after Chief Inspector Abberline had him arrested on charges of murder and badly beaten.

He gently touched my bruised cheek. "If not Sir Avery, how did ye get the guarantee for that amount of money?"

I saw as the answer came to him, that dark gaze narrowing. He slowly shook his head.

"You know," I told him. "*She* is quite fond of you, and there are the rumors..."

He shook his head. "Aye, that she is wealthier than the Queen. Do ye mean to tell me that these thieves now have her money?"

I managed a smile. "It is only important that they think they have the payment."

After everything the past months, that previous case, his anger when I left for Africa, my certainty that we were too different, that he didn't understand...

He did understand. And he had trusted me, although admittedly I should have told him about the amount I was going to bid to win that auction.

And more if necessary. It was the only way I saw of obtaining those documents.

"It worked," I said as he bent to cut the rope around my ankles.

"Aye, it worked."

"My bag?" Had it been lost when I was attacked by that 'mad butcher'?

"It is here, miss," Karl assured me. "It is good that I didn't have to make a choice to save you or the bag that is so important."

That could only have been something Brodie told him.

We spent the rest of the night in the baggage car as the train continued on to Paris.

There, we caught a connecting train to Calais where I made use of the accommodation facilities as best could be done on a rolling, rocking train. From there we caught the ferry across the channel, and a train from Dover back to London.

When we finally arrived, Karl Schneider immediately left to join his family, but not without enormous gratitude.

Brodie arranged to meet him the following day at the German Gymnasium, once Brodie had the opportunity to meet with Sir Avery. He'd keep his word that he would make certain Karl was allowed to remain in London.

We were both exhausted and bruised. Myself from that wagon ride across the city of Frankfurt to the rail station in time to take that last train of the night to Paris. Brodie from fighting his way out of the opera house after encountering two guards that one of the gentlemen bidders had sent after him.

I didn't want to go to the town house. There would have been too many questions from my housekeeper.

Nor was I ready to answer endless questions about the resolution of the case, most particularly that auction, from my great-aunt; there would be time enough for that later. Nor questions from Lily with her avid curiosity.

"Sir Avery?" I asked, as it was necessary for us to eventually meet with him in the matter of the case.

However, after sending Karl off to join his family, Brodie gave our driver instructions to take us to the office on the Strand.

Mr. Cavendish nodded a welcome, guarding the street entrance below should anyone arrive asking for either of us, while Rupert the hound settled himself outside the door to the office at the second-floor landing.

Once inside the office, Brodie poured some of my great-aunt's very fine whisky into two glass tumblers.

He emptied his glass and that dark gaze met mine.

"It's time to go to bed."

"It's barely past noon," I pointed out, hardly a respectable time to be abed.

He took my empty glass, set it on the table beside his, then took my hand as he led me to what served as a bedroom.

"There could be a scandal," I said then, my voice quite husky.

It could have been the whisky, that smothering ride rolled inside that filthy carpet on that insane trip across the city, or...that dark gaze that looked back at me now.

"Aye," he replied. "There could be. Do ye care?"

"Not at all," I replied.

Epilogue

WE HAD BEEN BACK in London almost a full month after returning from Frankfurt.

Brodie and I had met with Sir Avery and gave him our report about the case, emphasizing Karl Schneider's part in retrieving the documents. Brodie quite simply informed him that the least the Agency could do was to clear Karl to remain in the country. After all he was a skilled tradesman, and would be a loyal subject.

I had added that last part of our request, then informed Sir Avery that it was the least a grateful nation could do for someone who had acted selflessly and at great personal risk. In the end it was done.

"And the documents?" Sir Avery demanded with a look a Brodie.

That was the part of our report that did need some explanation.

According to what Brodie told him—and the story we had agreed upon—the design plans for an armed air ship that could rain devastation down on innocent people had been lost in a violent fire at the opera house in Frankfurt.

Only a slight embellishment. I had refused to see those documents, for what was obviously a weapon of war, handed over so the plans could become reality. Instead, I had convinced Brodie that they needed to be destroyed.

"If the bloody thing is not built now, another will take its place," he had pointed out. "Ye saw it yerself at the auction. All those very eager to have the plans, and with only one purpose for such a thing."

Precisely, I thought. But I was determined.

He was right, of course, and I knew it. It was the nature of despots, anarchists, and a past king or two. Power and greed.

Yet, I refused to be part of it, or to make such destruction any easier by returning the plans.

There was no need to explain further.

In the end, as we left the office on the Strand for that early morning meeting with Sir Avery that next day after our return. I had stopped at a steel barrel on the street where early morning workers in the East End huddled for warmth before starting their day. There, with Brodie's unspoken approval, I had tossed the entire set of documents into the fire.

I watched as the flames consumed them, with no small feeling of satisfaction, then explained that 'tragic circumstance' to Sir Avery later that same morning.

"Are ye satisfied now?"

"Yes."

"What do you mean that the documents were destroyed?" Sir Avery had demanded when informed about the 'fire.'

Brodie had explained the unfortunate 'circumstances' with amazing sincerity, that the documents had been lost 'in a fire at the opera house and it could not be prevented.' Most creative, I thought. I would have to be cautious with things he shared with me in the future.

"I would never lie to ye," he'd protested when I mentioned it. "Perhaps a wee stretch of the truth but only when necessary."

The little man who had attacked me in Brussels and accompanied Angeline Cotillard wherever she went, was the same one responsible for the murder of Sir Collingwood, and had stolen those plans. He was the one known as Szábo in that shadowy underground world.

The man Bruhl, whom no one had ever seen but was said to be responsible for stolen jewelry, a priceless artifact, and other documents—then sold to the highest bidder along with currency stolen from a French bank—was rumored in fact, to be a woman. Angeline Cotillard perhaps, posing as a man but never caught, when it suited the situation?

Most interesting. Although I was certain that she was very much a woman, evidenced by the portraits we had seen, an accomplished actress in disguise perhaps when it suited her. That might explain why Bruhl was never seen, or caught. Merely working behind the scenes.

She or he, as the case might be, had fled the auction that night after I stole the documents back. With nothing to sell, it seemed that she had simply vanished.

"The woman has apparently run to ground for the time being," Sir Avery had shared with us.

Her whereabouts were presently unknown, although it was thought that she would surface again to commit her next crime. And a warning that she would undoubtedly return to avenge Szábo's death.

"It seems the man was her brother. Hard to imagine," Sir Avery added. "But there you are and a word of caution."

Alex Sinclair was well on his way to full recovery from his wounds. He was particularly satisfied to learn that the little man whom we now knew as Szábo would not harm anyone else, as he had succumbed to his wound that night of the auction.

I should have felt some remorse. I did not.

There was understandably a scandal over the entire affair. Sir Collingwood had been highly revered among those in the military and with the royal family, in addition to his position as High Lord of the Admiralty.

His precise motive was not known. It was possible that he understood the very real danger of such a weapon and sought to balance the scales in some way, although that seemed contrary to his loyalty to the Crown.

Or perhaps, it was as simple as an affair. A man with no family who had dedicated his life to the military and then found it to be empty, and had found comfort as it were, with a woman who was an accomplished actress in *every* role she played and was able to persuade him to the dangerous scheme that cost his life.

We were informed that Sir Collingwood had been placed in an 'ice coffin' after his body was brought back to London, in consideration of his position until the case could be resolved. Quickly it was hoped.

Now that the inquiry was closed, he was to be buried in a simple, unmarked grave, as befitting the traitor that he had become.

The Prince of Wales had expressed his gratitude to Sir Avery for a job well done, the Crown protected, and for our efforts as well.

The royal family had then proceeded to cleverly excuse the

scandal as nothing more than an 'unfortunate situation,' as they had done in the past with other indiscretions.

As for the artist, Dornay, who was murdered in Brussels, we had recently learned that Angeline has been his muse from a very young age. That explained the portraits in his studio.

It was possible that the relationship had become far more. It wasn't unusual for the artist to fall in love with or become obsessed with the subject of his paintings.

Having seen Szábo's skill with the knife and very nearly experienced it firsthand, it was obvious that he had murdered the artist. But for what reason?

Jealousy perhaps? Or I suppose it was possible the artist had discovered Angeline's darker side, perhaps even her part in Sir Collingwood's death and had attempted to dissuade her from involving herself in any other such things? We might never know.

What I did know was that my agreement with Sir Avery had been satisfied. I was no longer obligated to assist in one of his schemes.

With our return, I had been pulled into our great-aunt's plans for my sister's wedding to James Warren. She was determined that it would be a grand affair, while Linnie wanted a simple, private ceremony.

She had been married before and suffered greatly for the scandal when it ended. For his part, Mr. Warren, my editor for my Emma Fortescue novels, chose to remain uninvolved as much as possible. Over a recent meeting to discuss my next book, I had congratulated him on a wise decision.

The wedding was to take place just before Christmas holiday, which was not far away. However, Linnie had indicated that they might prefer a simple appearance before a local magistrate. I was not about to step into that argument.

As for Brodie, he had been unusually subdued of late in spite of our recent 'resolution' of that very difficult situation between us that had me taking myself off on safari with my great-aunt and Lily. There did seem to be something bothering him.

I had arrived at the office on the Strand after spending the morning listening to my sister and our great-aunt discussing —bickering would be a better word for it—'the wedding.' I had finally abandoned them and fled—yes that was the correct word—to the relative sanity of crime and inquiry cases.

Brodie had looked up as I entered the office, that same preoccupied expression of the past week on his face. I might have thought it was some point of disagreement between us, except for the fact that I had spent most of the past week at Sussex Square with Lily, hiding out in the Sword Room.

There had certainly been no difficulty between us when I returned at the end of day and we shared supper, and other things.

It was then I suggested that we return to Old Lodge in the north of Scotland, distancing ourselves from Sir Avery and his suggestions of the work he wanted Brodie to take on next, wedding planning, and the frenzy my sister had worked herself into.

He had looked up then, and I thought there was almost a sadness there.

"Old Lodge?" he repeated, then took my hand. "Aye."

So here we were, having made the long train trip, mostly in silence with Brodie staring out the window of the compartment, while I made notes for my next novel with Emma

Fortescue stumbling upon stolen artifacts and a particularly handsome dark-eyed man.

I retrieved the bottle of whisky as he put another log on the fire in the hearth in the great room. I poured us each a dram, and then returned to the large sofa with down cushions that wrapped around one when they sat before the fire.

"There is something..." Brodie started to say, then stopped as he poked at the fire with the poker, sending sparks up the chimney in the large room with those large timbers overhead on the second floor.

I had always reminded me of some medieval hunting lodge, which it had been for at least a couple hundred years. Now it included that very lucrative whisky distillery in the adjacent long building.

"I want to tell ye..." He stood then and leaned against the timber mantel, staring down at the fireplace opening.

"About Rory."

I set my glass down on the side table.

Rory had been the young boy orphaned with the murder of his mother in that previous inquiry case. It had been a tragic affair, all the more so that it connected back to the ten-year-old murder of the young man she had an affair with. There was more however.

Brodie and the young woman had been together for a time before Stephen Matthews was found dead and the young woman accused of his murder. Brodie was certain she was not the murderer. With connections made over his time with the MET, he arranged for her to leave London to a place of safety.

Yet, when she returned all these years later, her life was in danger from that old case, and she had a child to protect.

When she was killed, Brodie had taken the boy, Rory, from

the scene of the murder and, as he had ten years earlier, sent him to safety, to give him time to find the actual murderer.

It had been a most complicated inquiry case, made all the more so with Brodie's certainty that Rory might very well be his own son.

He never had a family, with the death of his own mother in Edinburgh when he was a child, and he was determined that Rory would have the family that he himself had lost.

Stephen Matthews' own mother, still grieving the loss of her son all those years before, had taken Rory into her home and cared deeply for him. In the time since that case, Brodie had been a presence in the boy's life, with Adelaide Matthews' blessing.

It was as if it was a chance to make a difference in the boy's life, rather than see him cast out to the streets as he had been and left to survive on his own.

Now, it seemed this is what had him preoccupied the previous week, gone much of the time which I understood, then finally returning with that strange, almost sad expression in those dark eyes.

I had not attempted to interfere or persuade him to speak of whatever it was that obviously bothered him. That was not my way, as it was with some women I knew. Instead, knowing him quite well by now, I waited for him to share whatever it was that had created a new distance between us.

He was, after all, a Scot, and I had learned that no amount of prodding or persuasion would move him to speak of something until he chose to speak of it.

And now...

"I told ye that Ellie Sutton and I were together for a while," he began in a hesitant manner.

I nodded but said nothing. I sensed this was not a conversation.

"Ye knew there was a chance that I might be his father," he continued.

Once again, I said nothing as he struggled with whatever it was that he needed to say.

"The past months I was able to spend a good amount of time with him...Ah, lass, he is such a fine boy and he's been through so verra much."

He picked up his glass and took a long drink.

"Ye know what I feel for the lad."

I did, and I would have expected no less.

"I know yer heart, the kindness in ye along with the stubbornness and that temper of yers. And God knows yer intelligent and brave. It's what the boy needs after what he's been through. And I know ye said it didna matter to you that his mother and I were together before I knew ye. Yet, it's the reason I need to tell ye now..."

Author Note

So many new discoveries and other things, along with a few bodies...

Opium was not uncommon in the Victorian era even though it was banned in Britain in 1891 in an attempt to curb crime that went along with it, and found among all classes of society.

Lipstick as we know it was different. It was a combination of wax and color tint. In ancient times that tint came from a variety of natural sources—berries, and different plants. In the Victorian era it was seen primarily on actresses or other 'professional' women.

Air ships, the central element of the those stolen documents, had not yet been invented, but they were not far off, a predecessor to fixed-wing aircraft pioneered by Orville and Wilbur Wright, and others.

Passports as we know them were not issued until around 1914. However, there were 'Safe Conduct' papers issued by various countries for certain persons. But otherwise, people traveled freely for the most part from one country to the next in Europe.

The English language was spoken in many European countries, along with French (when in Paris), and in Brussels along with Dutch/Flemish.

Steamship and rail travel were wonderful innovations. I have carefully researched the travel times of the period: London to Dover, then to Calais, and on to Paris. Then additional travel for Brodie and Mikaela to Brussels and then on to Frankfurt. Beyond the cities, trains often traveled 200 miles more or less per day.

I've used German words and sayings that I'm familiar with, and many thanks to my fellow author, Virginie Marconato who lives in France, for her assistance with the French language where I've used it.

The reference to Charlemagne, King of the Franks in the Eighth Century, includes a fact I had not previously studied—that he led the Church Council to condemn Adoptionism, the concept that Jesus had been adopted by God.

Brodie and Mikaela will be pulled into a new murder in Book 10, *DEADLY LIES*, which will be very personal for both of them when Lily, whom they brought back from Edinburgh and is now part of their family, is drawn into the plot of a serial killer, and may become his next target.

However, as Brodie has often said, she is strong, fiercely independent, and a survivor much like Mikaela, and street-wise like Brodie. And she does have a fondness for swords. Then there is that question about young Rory Matthews to be answered. Who is his father?

Now, back to the computer, and thank you for coming along with two people who could not be more different.

Also by Carla Simpson

Revenge

Outlaws, Scoundrels & Lawmen

Desperado's Caress

Passion's Splendor

Silver Mistress

Memory and Desire

Desire's Flame

Silken Surrender

Angels, Devils, Rebels & Rogues

Ravished

Always My Love

Seductive Caress

Seduced

Deceived

About the Author

"I want to write a book..." she said.

"Then do it," he said.

And she did, and received two offers for that first book proposal.

A dozen historical romances later, and a prophecy from a gifted psychic and the Legacy Series was created, expanding to seven additional titles.

Along the way, two film options, and numerous book awards.

But wait, there's more a voice whispered, after a trip to Scotland and a visit to the standing stones in the far north, and as old as Stonehenge, sign posts the voice told her, and the Clan Fraser books that have followed that told the beginnings of the clan and the family she was part of...

And now... murder and mystery set against the backdrop of Victorian London in the new Angus Brodie and Mikaela Forsythe series, with an assortment of conspirators and murderers in the brave new world after the Industrial Revolution where terrorists threaten and the world spins closer to war.

When she is not exploring the Darkness of the fantasy world, or pursuing ancestors in ancient Scotland, she lives in the mountains near Yosemite National Park with bears and mountain lions, and plots murder and revenge.

And did I mention fierce, beautiful women and dangerous, handsome men?

They're there, waiting...

Join Carla's Newsletter

Printed in September 2024
by Rotomail Italia S.p.A., Vignate (MI) - Italy